SHAKEN

A QUAKE RUNNER: ALEX KAYNE THRILLER

KEVIN TUMLINSON

happy**pants**books

ALSO BY KEVIN TUMLINSON

Quake Runner: Alex Kayne

Shaken

Triggered (Forthcoming)

Citadel

Citadel: First Colony

Citadel: Paths in Darkness

Citadel: Children of Light

Citadel: The Value of War

Colony Girl: A Citadel Universe Story

Sawyer Jackson

Sawyer Jackson and the Long Land

Sawyer Jackson and the Shadow Strait

Sawyer Jackson and the White Room

Think Tank

Karner Blue

Zero Tolerance

Nomad

The Lucid — Co-authored with Nick Thacker

Episode 1

Episode 2

Episode 3

Watch for more at kevintumlinson.com/books

CHAPTER ONE

NOW | Houston, Texas

IT WAS *TECHNICALLY* STEALING.

Alexandra Kayne—call her *Alex*, or she probably wouldn't answer—had the usual moral and ethical qualms about taking things that didn't belong to her. But these days she tended to live by two core principles: *survive and, maybe more important, finish the job.*

She'd make up for the bad karma later.

When things settled down, and she was out of immediate danger, she'd make up for all of this. She'd send money. She'd make things right. Sometime, somehow, she'd balance the ledger.

For now, she had to do things the wrong way to get the right result.

She'd been spotted.

This job had required her to be exposed, if only briefly, and she'd gambled that she wouldn't be noticed. She'd lost that bet, and now she just had to get away from here as quickly as possible.

The job was done. It was time to run.

Across the street from the Ethos Software building was an upscale car wash—the type of place that had a comfortable waiting room, free WIFI, even free coffee and popcorn.

Why those two went so well together, Alex had never managed to guess. But these were strange times.

She liked places like this. They were on her "resource" list. Car washes, hardware stores, secondhand shops, resort hotel lobbies—when you were making do with whatever you had handy, places like these gave you plenty of options. Especially if you were willing to exercise some "moral flexibility."

She knew the clock was ticking. She needed to get as far away from here as she could, in the shortest time possible. But she needed a few things before she could make her exit.

She slipped out of the Houston heat and humidity and into the air-conditioned lobby of the car wash. The contrast was almost brutal—whatever the opposite of a surprise punch to the face might be, moving from outside to inside during a Houston summer was it.

She made a conscious effort to slow down, once inside, and to casually slip in alongside dozens of patrons who were milling about, inspecting various knickknacks and snack options. A large woman in a tank top and yoga pants was scrutinizing a rack of locally made fudge, and another gentleman in a camo T-shirt and cutoff shorts was reading a car magazine, lounging against the wall next to the rack.

Alex slipped past them, scanning the racks and shelves as she moved, looking for things that would be useful, resources that she could put to work if needed. She found several promising options.

Hanging from a peg in a slat-board display were several canisters of "Dog Repellant."

It was a way to skirt local laws about carrying pepper spray —a law that she thought was asinine, considering the rising rates of assault in the area.

She considered grabbing one of these, but decided against it. Pepper spray would mean being in proximity to her pursuers. If they were that close, she was already toast. She preferred evasion over conflict, when she could swing it.

Of course, when it came down to it, she didn't need pepper spray to defend herself.

Next she found a display of small tools, and among the hanging items was a small scraper—basically a razor blade stored in a flat plastic handle, meant for removing adhesive from glass.

She grabbed one of these.

Finally she moved to the display of novelty T-shirts and baseball caps, conveniently located near the rack of sunglasses. She snagged a blue T-shirt that read "I hit like a girl," with a picture of a broken baseball bat.

She liked the message of it, in context.

She also snagged a faux-distressed baseball cap with a tractor logo stitched to its front. The sunglasses were simple, black Rayban knockoffs. Nothing flashy, and nothing that would particularly stand out on a bright Houston day.

Perfect.

It was a small collection of items, and would have run her maybe $40 total, if she were planning to pay. Vastly over-priced, for sure, but not a fortune.

She had the money, but not the time. There was a line, as people waited to pay for their items or their car washes.

She also didn't want to linger near the register, where the

cameras would get a full-frontal shot of her. She could scrub that video later, but she wasn't entirely sure when she'd have time. Images might get out before she could get to them. Better to skip it.

She'd keep track. Send money later. Make it right.

As Alex moved deeper into the bustle of the carwash, she casually slid the razor blade from the plastic guard of the scraper and used it to cut the plastic tags from the hat and T-shirt. She left the debris, along with the scraper itself, in a small pile hidden behind a set of fairy-tale-themed coffee mugs. She rolled the cap up and shoved that in the left pocket of her jeans. The shirt she held like a rag as she moved, walking past the registers and deeper into the car wash waiting area.

The girl behind the counter was too busy working with the current customer to even notice her.

There were restrooms just past the vending machines, in a corridor that ran the length of the building. To her right was a long series of glass windows, beyond which several vehicles were slowly moving through powerful jets of water and beneath nozzles spraying multi-colored soap and wax.

There was a set of gun grips mounted to a pedestal along the inside of the windows, and a young girl was using them to aim a large squirt gun mounted outside, in the wash chamber. She was ecstatic about the stream of water hitting cars as they passed by and giggled with loud and adorable glee.

It might have made Alex smile any other time. As it was, it gave her a stab of nostalgia tinged by grief, over a life she wasn't likely to have. Connections lost, and opportunities taken from her.

If there was no time to buy overpriced car wash merchandise, there was certainly no time to grieve over a life that had been over for over almost two years now. She could moon over the idea of super adorable little girls once she was out of the soup.

The clock was still ticking.

She slipped into the restroom and locked herself in a stall, pulled off her shirt and replaced it with the new T-shirt, then pulled her hair into a ponytail and tucked it through the back band of the ball cap. The sunglasses completed the look —*modern soccer mom chic*—hiding her features in a screen of suburban camouflage most people wouldn't look at twice.

It should be enough.

Experience told her she could disappear this way, in plain sight.

As she opened the bathroom stall, Alex caught a quick glimpse of herself in the mirror. She looked cute. It was a far cry from the designer clothes and power blazers she'd worn just two years earlier. Trappings that she'd barely tolerated anyway —symbols of power and authority that were meant to distract people from the fact that she was a woman heading a technology business that was set to change the world.

Oh, and make billions.

The billions were sort of why she was here now, ducking into a restroom to pull on stolen car wash gear, on the run from what was just the most recent in a long string of attempts to put her in a cell somewhere, locked away tight and pressed to reveal a secret she just, frankly, was never going to reveal.

Billions could suck it.

She shoved her old shirt deep into the trash bin as she was leaving, piling paper towels and other garbage on top of it, and then stepped out into the long hall, moving along at the pace of the cars in the wash outside the window. Toward the exit.

Tick, tick, tick.

An automated door opened for her, and she stepped out once again into a shaded waiting area. A few other patrons lingered here, but made no attempt to talk to her or to each other.

The heat and humidity were still oppressive, despite the shade and even the faint breeze generated by two outdoor ceiling fans. No one else seemed even to notice the heat. They were used to it, maybe. Or they were impatient to get into their cars and get out of there.

Alex couldn't blame them—there were enough people out here, vying for shade, that it was difficult not to bump into each other. Somehow they managed, while hovering, waiting for one of the carwash employees to wave a towel and set them free.

That was the other good thing about car washes, Alex felt. Plenty of people, but everyone was focused on waiting things out so they could get moving. No eye contact. No chit-chat. No one looking at you and thinking maybe you look a little familiar. Everyone was more concerned with what to give as a tip than whether someone might be trying to hide from the police.

Alex moved to a corner of the shaded area and watched. Her clock was winding down, she knew. It would only be a matter of time before one of the agents involved in the raid at Ethos Software thought to look here, at the car wash across the street, to find the fugitive on the run.

If they came through before she'd managed her escape, things could get messy.

She didn't want to have to fight. She didn't want to risk hurting someone. She had a plan—hastily created, but workable. Things could go sideways, of course.

But that hadn't happened yet. Right now things were going pretty much according to the improvised plan. She was good. She was fine.

She just had to keep calm and keep watching.

One of the car wash workers looked up, scanning the patrons seated and standing in the shade. The worker waved his towel, indicating that the small Toyota pickup he'd been drying by hand was ready for its owner.

Alex glanced around and noted that no one was reacting. Those who did see him almost instantly looked back at their phones or whatever else had been occupying their attention.

This was her opportunity.

She moved forward, reaching into her pocket and taking out some cash. There was around $100 in tens and twenties in that stack, and she shoved all of it into the carwash guy's hand.

It was sort of a karmic gesture, to make up for the stuff she'd stolen—though she'd also pay that back, when she could. Also, she was about to do something to raise her karmic debt, and this was a way to at least get some goodwill into the mix.

But more than that, this was camouflage. The large tip distracted the man who had waved her over, and he didn't ask to see her receipt. A receipt she didn't have, of course.

He smiled and held the door for her.

The keys were in the visor. The radio was tuned to a Mexican radio station.

Alex returned his smile as she closed and locked the doors. She started the truck and put it in gear, moving out of the space and across the parking lot, turning onto the street.

She looked in the rearview mirror just in time to see two black sedans skid into the parking lot, and four men in dark suits hurriedly climb out and rush inside. They would lock the place down in a moment. Local police would be alerted to be on the lookout, but unless they'd spotted the Toyota leaving, they wouldn't know what to BOLO for, right away.

Alex had time—if she *took* her time.

No rushing. No erratic behavior. Just drive.

She kept to the speed limit, made the first turn she could, and then the next. She found an on-ramp to the highway. She used her signal as she merged with traffic. She kept to the right-hand lane and made no effort to pass any of the slower drivers.

She spent the next half hour moving at highway speeds in

as straight a line as possible before taking an exit and parking the Toyota in the shade behind one of the buildings in an abandoned car lot.

She put the keys back in the visor and found a rolled-up window shade in the floorboard behind the seat, unrolling it to place in the windshield. It would protect the truck from the heat and UV rays, but it was also a way to make it look less abandoned.

She dropped around five hundred dollars into the center console, made sure it wasn't visible from the outside, then locked the doors and closed them behind her.

Then she walked away.

The job was done. The client would be very happy—not to mention safe from any more harassment from Ethos Software's goon squad.

Her reason for being here, in Houston, was gone, and Alex Kayne could now move on to the next city, the next client. The next distraction.

The FBI could spend a few weeks looking for her in this area, if they wanted. Whatever made them feel productive.

She had another client, already waiting.

TWO YEARS EARLIER | SAN FRANCISCO, California

ALEX DIDN'T LIKE this part of the business. It felt like a perversion of what she'd had in mind, when she'd started all of this. She'd meant her work to keep people safe, to protect them from everything from identity theft to an intrusive and over-reaching government.

Now that very government was her biggest customer, and the majority of her work was labeled as classified.

The public might never even hear about it, much less benefit from it. If anything, the government would use her work to further erode the thin veneer of privacy left to the population.

This wasn't what she'd wanted *at all*.

Her partner, Adrian, couldn't have been happier, however.

"Cheer up!" Adrian said, pouring more than a couple of fingers of scotch from the wet bar. He beckoned with the bottle, and Alex shook her head.

"This contract has been amazing for the business," Adrian continued. "We've been able to do all those things on your bucket list, haven't we? We've helped a lot of people."

"Not as many as I'd hoped," Alex said. She stood up and moved to the large window that dominated an entire wall of Adrian's office. She had to admit the view from his space was much more impressive than it was from her own office. She hadn't cared which space she occupied when she took on the role of CEO of Populus. She was more concerned with building something on the foundation of the technology she'd invented, creating something that could change the world in profoundly positive ways.

The encryption tech was only a small part of the goals of the business. *Her* goals. Though she was starting to realize that she and Adrian didn't share those goals in common.

She should have seen it.

She was too in love with the idea of the good she could do in the world, and too blind to the ways her technology could be misused. Too blind to what was happening, right under her nose.

"The contracts have our tech locked up for two decades,

Adrian. *Twenty years* before the public can benefit from this. It's not what I wanted."

"What were you expecting?" Adrian asked, sipping his scotch. "Alex, you invented the *ultimate password breaker.*"

"It wasn't meant for that," Alex said, folding her arms over her chest and staring out at the city below. You could see the river from here, intersecting the park. It was a band of sparkling, dancing light. Alex considered it, wondering what it would be like to harness light in streams like that, to use it to move through the universe, to escape the limits of a world focused so entirely on profit that it couldn't even see the people below the line.

"It's what it ended up being used for," Adrian replied, snapping Alex away from that promising future and back to here and now. "QuIEK is the most advanced data encryption and decryption tool the world has ever known. You had to know the government would want to keep that close to their vests."

QuIEK, pronounced "quake" by its creator, was shorthand for "Quantum Integrated Encryption Key."

Adrian wasn't exaggerating when he trumpeted its power and benefits.

QuIEK was the most advanced system of its kind, able to lock data in such a way that it would take billions of computers billions of years to even get to the "enter your password now" stage. In fact, the only system in the known universe that could unlock a QuIEK-encoded file was QuIEK itself, along with whatever personal PIN or password or biometric security measure someone might have used to engage it.

If something was QuIEK-encoded, it could only be opened by whoever had locked it. Or whoever they entrusted it to.

But the same couldn't be said for any other form of encryption, quantum or otherwise.

That's where things got complicated. And a little scary.

Thanks to the AI framework and the quantum-computing aspects of the system, QuIEK was insanely compact. It could run on practically no resources whatsoever, while continuing to provide a level of computing power equivalent to every micro-processor ever made, working in tandem on the same problem, with unlimited resources behind the effort.

In other words, QuIEK was the most powerful system ever created. And its limits had yet to be determined—and might not even exist. No computer, no AI, no software ever created was its equal. Nothing humanity had ever built could match it, in terms of data encryption or, worse, data *decryption*.

Basically, QuIEK could walk through even the most advanced data security as if it wasn't there.

QuIEK could unlock *anything*.

No database, no password, no security system on the planet was immune to it. Which meant no government's secrets were immune to it.

Forget data privacy or security. Both concepts had just gone extinct.

Whoever controlled QuIEK controlled everything.

This was exactly what was giving Alex a lot of sleepless nights. She'd built QuIEK to help protect everyday people from an increasingly intrusive government, but also to guard against the more mundane threats that were becoming such a common occurrence in daily life. QuIEK would make identity theft and stolen credit card numbers and leaked passwords a thing of the distant past. Hazy memories, at best, from a dark era for online data and privacy.

That had been the idea, at least. That innocent, foolish, utterly naïve idea.

Adrian took up position next to Alex, looking out over the city below as if they were two rulers surveying their domain.

Except Alex had no desire for an empire. She'd wanted to

build something that made the world better. She'd wanted to build *lots* of things that made the world better. And because of this, because of her greatest work, everything else she'd hoped to do in the world was in jeopardy.

Maybe even the world itself.

It had become a very real possibility, she'd come to realize, that the tools she'd built could end up destroying the world she'd meant to save.

"So the deal is they want us to shut down all other operations," Adrian told her, sipping again from his scotch. "Too many variables to control. Too many opportunities for leaks or security breaches. To compensate, the contract they're offering us pays nearly six times our annual revenue." At this Adrian grinned. "More money than we even projected in our ten year figures, Alex. More money than we ever dreamed. And all we have to do is keep developing and improving QuIEK."

"For them," Alex said. "For the government."

"They're going to take it anyway," Adrian said, shrugging. "If we don't agree to these terms, they'll shut us down, lock us into confidentiality agreements if not a couple of small and windowless rooms. And they'll take QuIEK anyway. This deal makes us rich, at least."

"And completely robs us of any freedom to make anything else. It's a bad deal."

"It's the *only* deal," Adrian said, his voice hard.

Alex thought about it, looking out over the city.

She had worked her whole life for two things: Complete independence, and the ability to make a better world. Now, both of those were being ripped away from her, and she was being told that her only choice was to take it.

She was being told that what she built wasn't hers, that it had always been up to others what she could do or build or keep.

Or who she could help.

"No," she said, her voice quiet but firm.

Adrian was staring out at the landscape. "No," he repeated quietly, ironically. Then he nodded. "I get it, Alex. I've known you longer than just about anyone. I get it. You can't stand the idea of someone telling you what you can and can't do."

"That's not it," Alex said, shaking her head.

"You can't stand anyone controlling any aspect of you, telling you that you have to stay in a box. That you have no say," Adrian said, his expression twisted into a look of complete disdain.

Alex said nothing, because there was nothing to say.

"But this is what it *is*, Alex. This is the *US government* telling you that you're in a box. So you'd better make it as comfortable as possible. Otherwise they'll put you in a different box, where you can rot for all they care."

Alex understood this, but it didn't matter. "I won't let them take it, and I won't let them tell us what we can do as a business. That isn't going to happen."

Adrian laughed, and it was a sharp and bitter sound that made Alex feel a sick twinge. "And what the hell are you going to do about it, exactly? It's *done*, Alex! I..."

He hesitated. Then shook his head, clearly deciding there was no point in putting it off. "I signed the contract this morning."

Alex looked at him sharply. "You what? You don't..."

"Have the right?" Adrian laughed. "The authority? Read my contract again, Alex. I'm one of two people in this company who has decision making power at that level. Me and you. And our advisors back me."

"They're not a board of directors," Alex said. "This is a private company. *My* company."

"I know," Adrian waved, dismissive. "A private company

with an even more private owner," he sneered. "But the investors own a large enough percentage, along with mine, to make this happen. And it *has* happened. It's done."

Alex turned and studied her friend—her oldest friend—and felt sick.

Not because she'd been betrayed. She'd known that Adrian was set to turn against her in this, at some point. He'd been pushing for a deal like this almost since QuIEK was invented.

It was Adrian who had started all of these wheels in motion in the first place. Alerting the government, proposing deals and contracts, agreeing to concessions. Alex knew all of that, despite Adrian's attempts to hide it. Adrian had betrayed her a long time ago.

No, Alex felt sick because of what she was about to do to Alex, and to their advisors, and to Populus—the business they'd built together, in the name of what she'd always believed was a just and righteous mission.

She felt sick because of her own impending betrayal.

She checked her smart watch, and saw the notification there, waiting. The events she'd put into motion were ready for her. All it would take was a touch.

She touched the watch, and everything started.

She turned away with Adrian still staring out at the landscape. Her friend was thinking that he'd won, she knew.

Alex, on the other hand, was thinking she wanted to get to the ground floor before the automated systems shut down the elevators for good.

The deadlock would be a cascade of shutdowns, with the elevators being the last to go, and only once the AI monitoring system determined they were empty.

But it would be a fairly rapid shutdown. Everything was about to go offline. She needed to be at ground level before that happened.

In the private, executive parking section of the garage, Alex climbed into her silver Tesla. She paused only long enough to let out the breath she'd been holding.

Then she started the Tesla and sped away from the building that she'd more or less thought of as home for most of the last decade. She'd just spent the last moment there. She'd never see it again.

Soon, it wouldn't even exist.

Her phone rang, and she answered, already knowing who it would be and what it would be about.

"Alex, *what did you do!*" Adrian shouted, panicked. "Everything... everything's shutting down! Everything in the system is gone!"

"It's not gone," Alex replied. "It's locked."

There was a pause. "Wait... did you... did you use QuIEK? Did you just lock us out of our own systems?"

"For good," Alex said. "All the data, all the research, everything that was QuIEK, it's all locked in our systems. You'd need QuIEK itself to unlock it. That, and my personal access code. It's finished, Adrian. The government will just have to learn to deal with it."

"*You idiot!*" Alex shouted. "You've killed us! *You've killed us!*"

"Adrian, relax. The US government isn't going to take out a hit on us over this. At most they'll imprison me and try to force me to unlock the data. They..."

"It's the *Russians*, Alex!" Adrian shouted into the phone.

She paused. Blinked. "What?" Alex felt herself go cold. "What are you talking about, Adrian? What did you do?"

There was the sound of heavy breathing over the phone, and Adrian finally responded. "I cut a second deal. Under the table. I... I sold QuIEK to the Russians. It's a secret. Something I've been working on for months, since they approached me."

He laughed. "Approached me," he said again, an ironic note in his voice. "They didn't give me a choice, Alex. They want to... they're going to use this for disinformation, and for cracking US security. They're here, in the building. I was on my way to meet with them when... when everything went *crazy*."

Alex felt her own breathing increase, her pulse pounding in her throat. "No, Adrian, you didn't. How could you?"

"I told you, I had no choice! I couldn't say no! But it was more than that, Alex. It was... it was *money*. More money than you've ever imagined! Money enough to buy our own country, for God's sake! By the time they brought the US down, we could be anywhere in the world. We could be anyone. We could be..." He didn't finish, and Alex didn't bother trying to imagine whatever twisted fantasy he'd concocted.

He was delusional.

Insane.

She hadn't let herself believe it until this moment, but it was clear.

"But now," Adrian said. "Now..."

"Now they'll kill us," Alex said. "Or worse."

"Worse? What could possibly be worse?"

Before Alex could answer a truck in the oncoming lane swerved toward her. She reacted quickly and on instinct, slamming the wheel to the right and spinning the Tesla sideways. The maneuver itself saved her, kept her from a head-on impact, but she didn't have the speed. She couldn't avoid the crash entirely.

The truck clipped the driver's side, just behind her seat, sending the Tesla into a spin and slamming Alex against the door.

The airbags deployed, and Alex was slammed backwards and sideways all at once. She felt something give in her ribs, followed by a sharp pain.

At some point in the chaos the car stopped moving, and Alex heard the sounds of the city, people stopping and exiting their own vehicles, concerned, already calling for emergency services. There was a ticking noise from under the dash of the Tesla, and Alex noted it but couldn't place what it was. Everything seemed slowed, including her own thinking.

She was dazed, not sure what was happening and what to do about it. The airbags sagged, and she looked up to see someone exiting the truck, looking completely unfazed and moving with hardened purpose.

He had something in his hand.

A gun.

Alex had no time. She had to think of a way out of this. She knew, mostly by instinct, what was coming next.

The Tesla was dead on the street and not going anywhere. The man was approaching, weapon in hand, and it was clear what was coming next. Alex frantically ran the situation through her mind, looking around in her mental landscape at her inventory of resources.

There were always resources.

Everything she needed.

Everything you need is right in front of you, her grandfather's voice was saying, echoing around inside her head.

Everything she needed.

Everything was...

She reached out to the dash and took her phone from the magnetic mount. She held this up to the window, pushing it against the glass with a click. The move was so unusual and unexpected it made the gunman pause.

"If you shoot me," Alex said. "Your bosses will never get the key. Only the US government will have it, and Mother Russia will forever lose its place on the world stage overnight. *All your secrets are belong to us!*"

Big talk. And possibly a corny pop-culture reference that might go right over the guy's head—she couldn't be sure in her current state.

It was also a total bluff. The US government had nothing, and never would.

The gunman might be fully aware of that. His presence here meant that someone had been monitoring them closely. The Russians that Adrian had planned to meet with, the ones that were in the building when Alex had shut everything down, had clearly had someone watching her, following as she'd left Populus.

They might know everything. They might be fully aware that Alex had quantum locked QuIEK itself. This might be Alex's last day on Earth.

The gunman quickly glanced around, then yanked open the door of the Tesla, with the sound of wrenching, anguished metal. He grabbed the phone from Alex's hand and then grabbed Alex herself. He yanked her out of the car, barely letting her unbuckle her seatbelt first.

Another car squealed to a stop, and the gunman shoved Alex inside before climbing in beside her.

In seconds they were racing away from the scene, and Alex marveled at the irony of being safe and completely screwed at the same time.

CHAPTER TWO

NOW | ORLANDO, Florida

SMOKESCREEN WAS what made all of this possible.

For the past two years, Alex had meticulously built the network, traveling from city to city and town to town, scouting any open WiFi hotspots that she could exploit. If she couldn't find an open signal, she'd use QuIEK to make one, connecting her "bots" in a way that was practically invisible on the network. She always and only used public places with lots of foot traffic. Zebra stripes to confuse any lions who might be lurking.

The bots were little microcomputers built from readily available kits she could pick up from hobby shops and electronic retailers nearly everywhere. Each bot ran an open-source operating system and remote desktop software. They were cheap, disposable computers that were also tiny and easy to hide right out in the open. Their power consumption was low, and it was easy to make them look like part of the scenery.

Alex would scout a location and build the bots to look like they were just another gadget or gizmo linked to the utilities or security systems or electrical fixtures of a small business. She would hijack power from other systems nearby, using it to charge a backup battery as well as power the system itself.

Smokescreen allowed her to log in to any one of thousands of these bots in cities and towns all over the country. It was how she could be in Cornswallow, Texas and appear to be in LA, Manhattan, or Denver on any given day, or even hour by hour.

Anyone who might be looking for her online would have a difficult time of it. Even if they staked out the coffee shop or bar or grocery store where she appeared to be, she'd "exit" unseen, and be a thousand miles away—virtually speaking—the next time she logged on. In reality, she might still be in the same Airbnb or hotel room she'd been in for weeks.

Alex knew that tracing her online wasn't something that happened often. She had unfettered access to every network of every agency that was on her tail. She could see the progress of their manhunt, and though they were sometimes a little close for her comfort, the near misses usually came more from them getting lucky and her getting sloppy—either by accident or out of necessity.

If she played it smart, she could be invisible forever.

The problem was, she sometimes couldn't play it smart. Sometimes the job made it impossible to stay off the radar.

This last gig had been one of those, and she was still freaking out about it, just a little. By now she'd managed to put quite a bit of distance between her and that car wash, had switched vehicles half a dozen times, and had left some virtual breadcrumbs to lead the Feds in the opposite direction. It hadn't entirely worked—they'd assumed that anything digital would be compromised, which was smart of them. But it delayed them briefly, each time, which was all Alex needed.

She felt safe enough for now. Which was to say she was in a public place where she could blend in and be anonymous while using a VPN to remote into a Smokescreen bot in another state, while keeping an eye on all the exits locally.

It was about as safe as she could expect these days, but it had served her well, so far.

At the moment, she was in Orlando, and she was preparing to meet with a new client.

The client entered through the front door of the restaurant. And she wasn't hard to miss. She was attractive, but that wasn't what caught the eye of everyone as she walked in.

It was her arm.

The obviously missing arm.

She seemed self conscious and alert all at once, but once she spotted Alex's smartwatch on the edge of the table, the signal they'd arranged in advance, she put her head down and moved quickly. She stopped in front of the booth. "Are you..." She hesitated, as if uncertain how to put it. "I'm looking for someone."

"Some people say I'm a someone, Abbey," Alex said, smiling and motioning for her to take a seat.

Abbey eyed the room, looking around nervously, which was something Alex really wished she would not do. But most of the patrons were doing their best not to look at her, or not to look at the stump of her left arm.

Deformity, Alex mused, *might just be the best camouflage.*

She doubted anyone in the room could describe Abbey or pick her out of a lineup, other than to say she was missing an arm. Alex filed this away as a useful bit of information to add to her resource list—that growing mental database of handy things to know, just in case.

Of course, she'd rather not *actually* lose an arm, just to keep hidden. But she could always fake it.

Ponder this later, she chided herself. *Work now*.

She focused on what she knew about the client, waiting for Abbey to relax enough to talk, to answer questions, and to receive some instructions.

Abbey Cooper. Twenty-five years old, and a fairly recent graduate of the University of Florida. She was a transplant to Orlando, having moved here for school after spending the first 18 years of her life in Dallas, Texas. She had graduated in the top five of her class and had entered college life with a resume stuffed with AP classes and a couple of scholarships to pay most of her way. She worked for the rest, primarily with paid research jobs that were a bonus part of her program.

She wanted to be a marine biologist—a career that she'd stuck with even after losing her arm in a shark attack.

Alex really liked the girl's obvious character and strength, even in the face of pain and challenges. She liked Abbey's dedication. It made Alex want to help her all the more.

Abbey settled into the booth, practically collapsing in on herself. She sat with her head down and her single arm in her lap, as if the missing one might have been folded over it. She wouldn't make eye contact.

"It's ok," Alex said. "You don't have to be afraid. I'm here to help."

Abbey looked up at her then, a curious expression on her face, as if she couldn't figure out what she was seeing across the table from her. "How?" she asked. "How could you help? I've been to the police, to the FBI, even another private investigator..."

"I'm not a private investigator," Alex said calmly, correcting.

She shook her head. "Right. How... how did you hear about me again?"

"I learned about you from the FBI," Alex said, a little elusive.

It was true, strictly speaking. Using Smokescreen and QuIEK, Alex had found Abbey's file languishing in the FBI's caseload database, untouched for more than six months now. It was how she found the majority of her clients—the hopeless souls suffering injustice from criminals and inaction from authorities.

It wasn't the FBI's fault, of course. They had only limited resources, and some cases became low priority out of necessity. Important—every case was important. But perhaps not as important as preventing terrorist attacks or shutting down human trafficking networks.

There always seemed to be resources enough to keep the hunt for Alex Kayne going, though. And Alex felt some responsibility for that. If the FBI was putting resources into finding her, then those resources weren't available for helping people like Abbey Cooper.

That was an injustice, Alex felt. A karmic debt she was ultimately responsible for creating. She had to do something to balance that out.

"They said they'd run out of leads," Abbey said almost absently, staring out of the booth and at the large windows across the way.

The view wasn't anything particularly interesting. It was largely the curved drive leading up to the valet lane of the restaurant, and beyond that was the roadway, busy with traffic conveying people to whatever their daily lives happened to be, here.

This restaurant was just off the lobby of a hotel and was filled with people laying over temporarily before slipping out to go to Disney World or board a cruise ship or whatever pleasures awaited them. Hotel lobbies and hotel restaurants were on Alex's resource list, valuable for their anonymity but also for the plethora of resources they provided in the form of amenities, such as internet-connected computers and free WiFi.

And sometimes fruit and infused water, which was also handy.

"They're definitely out of leads," Alex said to her. "Which is why I reached out to you. And I'm going to ask you to keep quiet about our meeting and about me helping you. Consider it payment."

She shook her head. "That's the other thing. I don't have any money. I have a job, but it's barely paying the bills right now. So I'm not sure..."

"You've been covered," Alex said.

It was a half truth.

In reality she didn't need Abbey to pay her because she really didn't need money. Not much money, anyway.

Her needs were slight. She could get by on very little, most of the time, and she actually had stockpiles of cash stashed in lockers and drops all over the country. She also had dozens of prepaid credit cards with thousands of dollars on each of them.

Having unlimited access to the systems used to move money around, globally, had its perks. Alex made sure that any funds she needed were transferred from people and businesses that seemed determined to do nasty things in the world.

Still... she didn't get greedy. And she didn't use this reach to mete out justice. She might have the ability to bankrupt a corrupt CEO or mafia boss, but she didn't have the right. That wasn't how justice worked.

Of course, her definition of justice wasn't entirely in line with anyone else's either. She operated with scruples and a code, if for no better reason than to make sure she didn't cross a line and become someone she hated.

It was a quirky sort of balance to strike.

Alex knew that Abbey couldn't afford to pay her, anyway. She never asked clients to pay.

The job wasn't about making a living. It was about having a purpose.

"I'm going to solve this problem for you, and all I'm asking is that you never tell anyone how it was resolved. You never tell anyone about me. Deal?"

Abbey blinked and shook her head. "I don't actually know anything about you, anyway."

"There isn't that much to know. I was like you, once. I was let down by the system that was supposed to protect me. No one helped me. I didn't like it. So now I help when I can, because no one should have to accept injustice as inevitable."

Abbey was staring at her, and finally she smiled a little and laughed. "You sound like someone out of a movie. You just show up and right all the wrongs, like a superhero or something?"

"I'm just someone trying to help," Alex replied, smiling. "No real super powers, unless you count being a good listener. Now, let's talk about what happened to you."

ABBEY COOPER HAD one of the more unusual stories that Alex had ever heard. Which made what happened to her feel all the more tragic and infuriating.

The shark attack, less than two years earlier, felt like the end of everything for her at the time. It had certainly been an abrupt and horrific ending to what she'd thought of as a big step in her career.

Abbey and a few of her friends had been lucky enough to be picked for a trip to Kauai, in the Hawaiian islands. They were part of a research team, studying the local sea turtle population, largely doing the grunt work, though doing so on white sandy beaches and in the bright blue ocean waters surrounding the island.

The research was serious business, and the students were honored to have their spots. But everyone, instructors and researchers included, recognized that this was a coveted opportunity to spend some time in paradise.

There was plenty of time for fun.

The atmosphere in the research camp was always light and energetic, something of a party atmosphere as long as the work was done on schedule. Many of the researchers had become accomplished surfers over years spent on the islands.

Abbey and the others had taken up the sport themselves, and spent hours in the waves, between shifts, learning to balance and steer and read the waves. She was getting pretty good at it, she thought, and even managed to buy her own board—second hand, but beautiful.

They also spent hours diving. Abbey had gotten her SCUBA certification months earlier and was glad to put it to work in such a pleasant spot. She was one of several divers at the camp, and when she wasn't on duty she and a few friends would dive just for fun, exploring the reefs and rocks, even playing tag with some sea turtles, who seemed to recognize them as friends.

It was a glorious, charming world under the water. Abbey had dreamt of just this sort of life since she was a little girl standing next to the glass walls of the aquariums at SeaWorld, in San Antonio.

She'd dreamt of being right here, surrounded by blue water and sea life, swimming along with it, as if she were a part of it.

It was during one of these excursions that Abbey had been attacked.

Tiger sharks were not unusual in the area. Everyone had

been warned to be on the lookout. There'd been some scattered reports of sightings, though they'd mostly been miles down the coast. Still, they were warned often that the turtles made for tempting prey, and the sharks themselves could be indiscriminate about what they consumed.

Abbey had been with two other research assistants, accomplished divers themselves, and the three of them had taken one of the small motor boats out to a nearby reef, where they could see all manner of tropical fish and other aquatic life. They'd been in the spot for a couple of hours, and the signal had gone out that it was time to get back to the boat.

Abbey had been admiring a colorful fish that had nosed her hand and toyed with her, playful and curious. She gave it a tiny wave goodbye, and it suddenly darted away into the reef.

She kicked once, aiming for the surface, and suddenly felt something slam into her from behind.

The force of it had masked what had really happened for a few seconds. It had dazed her, put her in a bit of shock. But as the waters clouded with her own blood, she became aware of what it was, and panicked.

She kicked frantically, unthinking, simply trying to get back to the boat that had already been her destination. The shark, which had only taken a nip on its first pass, came at her again. This time it intended to feed.

In a single bite it was over. Abbey had felt it, felt the sharp puncture of it, the stinging and burning and tearing sensation of it.

And then she was gone.

She awoke on the deck of the boat as it was speeding to the shore. One of her friends hovered over her, though she wasn't sure which friend it was. She wasn't sure of anything at all, except that she felt strangely numb, and bizarrely calm. She knew, somewhere in her darkening mind, what had happened.

She sensed it. But it seemed surreal. It seemed distant. And she faded out of consciousness again, thinking only of the small, colorful fish she'd waved to as she'd started her ascent.

Again she awoke, this time in the hospital, on a gurney being rushed through the ancient and dingy looking halls. Above her there were alternating patches of light and dark as the gurney passed under the fluorescent lighting. There was something on her face, and she reached up to move it—and nothing.

Nothing happened.

No touch of her fingers, no grasping, no resistance from a restraint.

Someone—a nurse, she thought—stepped in beside her and pushed the plunger on a syringe, attached to a length of clear tubing.

For the third time, the world went dark.

And when she'd awoken, her life had changed.

Her left arm had been taken from just above the elbow, leaving a mutilated stump that was a mockery of everything she'd ever wanted out of life. All the dreams of work in the oceans, all the plans to move forward in this career—it all seemed like a joke now. The cruelest joke.

She'd lost more than 60 percent of her blood in the attack. She was lucky to have survived at all, they told her. Lucky she'd been as close to the boat as she'd been. Lucky the shark had broken off pursuit. Lucky they were able to get her to the hospital so quickly, that there was a match for her blood type on hand, that the bite had been on her arm rather than her torso.

Lucky.

The arm—the *missing* arm—still had sensation. She could still feel it there. Mostly she felt the pain of it.

Cramped muscles in her hand, strain in her forearm.

Phantom pain, they told her. They gave her drugs, which helped. But nothing really made any of it better. Nothing made her feel whole. She was less than she'd been before she'd gone on that dive. Less than she'd been when she dreamed of a life among creatures of the sea—creatures like the turtles, that colorful little fish, and the shark itself.

She was less of who she was, physically and mentally. And she knew that would be true for the rest of her life.

She cried. She grieved. She became angry. She grieved some more.

Time passed, and she began slowly to recover. Physically, at least. And with that recovery, she came to realize that she was now, somehow, something of a celebrity.

Her attack, it turned out, had been in the same region in which professional surfer Bethany Hamilton had suffered a strikingly similar attack while surfing with friends, losing her own arm to a tiger shark's bite. Hamilton had gone on to write a book about her experiences, from the shark attack to returning to the water and, seemingly against all odds, becoming a champion surfer. That book had become a hit film, and Abbey remembered seeing it, flinching in horror at the idea of something so horrible happening, and then...

And then crying, tears of joy, when Hamilton succeeded. She remembered marveling over how Hamilton could have even gone back into the water, facing the same waves where she'd lost her arm. And not only facing them down again, but *conquering* them.

It just seemed so inspiring.

And so impossible.

The parallels in their two stories, following Abbey's attack and her subsequent recovery, had resulted in some national media attention and a great deal of public support. She'd even met Bethany Hamilton herself, who had posed with Abbey for a photo series that had gone viral. Abbey, still horrified by the loss of her arm, had barely managed to smile in the photos, and her eyes were rimmed with tears. This seemed to draw even greater sympathy from the public, and a Kickstarter campaign was formed.

"An Arm for Abbey" was a crowd-funded endeavor to get Abbey a prosthetic arm. And not just *any* prosthetic.

Supporters raised more than a million dollars on Abbey's behalf, in just under thirty days, as a way to get her into an experimental prosthetics program. With the donations going to funding the research, Abbey was shortlisted as a recipient for a new and highly advanced prosthetic limb that utilized a combination of AI and neural-muscular integration. It was the first of its kind.

Once accepted into the program, however, the real work—and the real pain— began.

Receiving the prosthetic required Abbey to undergo implant surgery. Doctors inserted a metal post and receiver into the bone of her arm and reorganized the nerves from her stump. They created contact points for sensors, and implanted advanced digital sensors that could not only interface with the new arm but would allow Abbey to experience actual sensation and pressure. She would also experience nearly eighty percent of the manual dexterity of a real arm—a percentage, she was told, that would increase over time, as she used the arm more frequently, learning how to interface with it as it learned how to interface with her right back.

The surgeries were painful—excruciating, at times. Recovery was long and grueling. Abbey cried often, as much from frustration as from the pain and effort. But she endured. She learned. Her acuity increased, and eventually the pain... stopped.

Even the phantom pain.

Somehow, through this new neural link, through the tactile feedback she received from millions of artificial "nerves," through the virtual experience of regaining her arm, she was somehow "healed."

In other words, it was a miracle.

And one that Abbey had been incredibly grateful for. With her new arm she was able to resume much of her life as it had been. She could cook, clean her apartment, even drive. She could touch type again, albeit slower and more deliberate than she had before, but the capability enabled her to complete her graduate thesis and graduate with a Master's in Marine Biology. It had enabled her to complete the requirements for acceptance in to the PhD program.

And over time, her speed and accuracy increased.

It was like learning to play an instrument or acquire a new skill. The more she did it, the more her brain rewired itself to accommodate this strange, artificial limb. And the limb, in turn, was learning how to work for her, as well.

The AI built into the prosthetic was the truly experimental part of the technology. It represented a leap forward in human-technology hybridization. Essentially, the arm had its own "brain," composed of a series of nanotube "neurons" that could form, reform, reshape, and realign themselves. Similar to the way the human brain's neurons fired and wired together, the nanotube neurons would align to better accommodate repeated patterns and signals from Abbey's brain.

It was learning her as much as she was learning it.

The result was that Abbey's life was slowly getting back on track.

She had effectively picked up where she'd left off, perhaps a bit encumbered but less so than she'd been before. The arm was definitely a miracle. It gave her back autonomy and independence. It not only gave her life back, it made her new life possible.

And then, one day, it was gone.

The batteries in the arm could sustain operation for 24 hours, but to ensure it didn't suddenly stop working when it was needed, it had to be charged regularly. And so, each evening Abbey removed the arm and then plugged it in and left it on the dresser in her room, so it could charge as she slept. Every morning she would awaken and shower and prepare for the day, and then reattach the arm before leaving her bedroom. The charge would last all day, and even all night, but this routine made sure it was always ready. She even had a spare battery pack if she needed it.

For months now, her routine had been to wake up, get ready, and then attach the arm before getting to the rest of her day. She'd become adept at grooming with just her right arm—something she did as a way to remind herself that she was *capable*, and the arm was just a tool. A wonderful tool, but not required for her to live her life.

Still, she always looked forward to attaching the arm, to feeling the little tingle and pulse as it activated and came alive, joining her biological nervous system as a welcome extension. It was the favorite part of her morning.

But on this particular morning, her hair still damp and a towel wrapped around her, she came out of her bathroom to discover that the arm and its charging system were gone.

Someone, somehow, had entered the apartment with neither her nor her roommate noticing, and stolen the prosthetic.

Abbey had called the police immediately. She'd also called Uconic Prosthetic Technologies, the company that had built the arm. The arm was still experimental, and Abbey was technically assisting in the testing and perfecting of the technology.

She was required to bring the arm in once every two weeks so Uconic's researchers could download data and make any adjustments or upgrades.

They would need to know that, somehow, Abbey had lost their experimental technology.

News of the theft had set off a chain reaction within the company. They had immediately hired private investigators to assist in the investigation, and Abbey had met with them dozens of times to answer questions. She'd done the same for the police and then, unexpectedly, for the FBI.

Uconic had government contracts, she learned. The prosthetics program was under the umbrella of military research. She was a test subject, helping them perfect the technology for military as well as civilian applications. As such, the stolen tech was a big deal.

For Abbey, it was worse.

The stolen arm meant a loss of mobility. It meant being *limited* again, having to work twice as hard to do the same tasks. It meant being reminded of what she'd lost, again and again, every time she had to struggle with a task as simple as tying her shoes.

But it also meant suspicion.

Uconic's government contracts made the tech in the arm a sensitive secret, and that meant the FBI had to treat it as potential espionage. Suddenly Abbey found her life being turned upside down by intrusive questioning, by requests for bank records, by limitations on her travel and even on her internet access. She'd suffered through a brief house arrest as they'd gone through her life with a microscope, looking for any hint that she might have colluded with a foreign agent.

Abbey had suffered through all of this alone, because she wasn't allowed contact with her own family or friends during this time. Even her roommate was relocated briefly—presumably undergoing the same sort of scrutiny.

During one of the most vulnerable times of her life, she was being treated as if she might be a criminal. And when she was finally cleared, she was warned that they'd still be watching, and worse, that she would not receive another prosthetic from Uconic.

She might be cleared of any criminal activity, but she was treated as if she were guilty anyway, for having allowed the arm to be taken.

"Why give it to me in the first place, if it was such a big secret?" Abbey asked, tears in her eyes. She dabbed at them with a tissue that Alex handed her.

"Field tests," Alex said. "They needed data on how the arm performed in real-world scenarios. They would likely have taken it back eventually, Abbey. I'm sorry."

She shook her head. "It's just so... unfair."

Alex agreed. It *was* unfair. It was *unjust*.

What they'd done to Abbey was wrong in every way Alex could think of. And she couldn't help seeing parallels to her own situation. The government contract, the grab for technology that could help everyday people, the attempt to lock it down as a government secret.

The victim blaming.

"I'm going to help you," Alex told her, reaching out a hand across the table and resting it on Abbey's own.

"How?" Abbey asked, her lips trembling from the emotion of it all. "Even if you find out who took the arm, they'll never give it back to me. I'll still be..."

She didn't finish, but simply raised the stump of her arm. Alex could see the cylindrical metal receiver, where the arm would have attached, along with the nodules used to connect her nervous system to the arm's AI.

It gave Abby a strangely *unfinished* look—much more so than the stump itself would have given her. To Alex it looked like a broken promise, as if Abbey had been told that her life would be put back together, and then all of it was left half done.

Alex shook her head. "Abbey, I'll be honest with you. Right this second, I have no idea how I'll fix this. But there's a balance that needs to be restored here. They promised you an arm. That's something I'll have to work out. But they also treated you like you were the criminal in this, and that's something I'll definitely settle up with them. I don't know how. Not yet. But that's my job, to figure it out. Ok?"

Abbey was looking down at the table, and nodded. "Ok," she said quietly. She looked up then. "But if you don't want me to pay you, why are you helping?"

Alex smiled. "It's my job. Also, I've been where you are. And it sucks. Don't worry. I never leave a job unfinished. That's my rule. I'm in this with you, til the end. I'll figure out how to make this right."

She stood and left cash to pay for their meal and drinks. She smiled at Abbey one last time.

"It's what I do."

CHAPTER THREE

TWO YEARS EARLIER | San Francisco, California

THEY HAD her hands bound behind her, zip-tied tight enough that her fingers tingled. They spoke Russian, and Alex had no clue what they were actually saying, but their tone was clear enough.

Wherever they were taking her, it was going to be unpleasant.

They'd taken her phone, but they hadn't searched her. She couldn't really know their reasoning, but she could guess.

She was a woman. Unlikely to have anything in her pockets at all, much less something that would create problems for them.

They were wrong about that.

Her grandfather's Swiss Army knife was slender and nearly flat. It was basic, with just a blade, a screwdriver that doubled as a bottle opener and a can opener. There were tweezers and a plastic toothpick in the handle. She carried it in her front right pocket, and liked it for being flat and unobtrusive.

Even with her hands bound it was easy enough to slip the knife out of her pocket and open the blade. Angling it so that she could cut the zip ties without slicing her wrists was more challenging, particularly in a moving vehicle. But after a moment she had the blade under the plastic and was able to twist and move to give herself the leverage she needed.

The blade cut through the plastic in a smooth slice, with only slight resistance. She kept her hands together and hid the open knife against her palm. She had to think about what to do next.

The two Russians were in the front seat of the sedan, chatting and occasionally laughing. After they'd bound her, the Russian who had rammed the truck into her had gotten into the front seat, where he and his partner chatted amicably. Oblivious.

They didn't consider her a threat, and so they paid little attention to her.

Alex glanced around, looking for the resources, and decided on a plan that made her just a little squeamish but would give her the best chance of survival. She took a few breaths, calming herself, and then waited for them to stop for a light. She counted down, and the moment the driver hit the accelerator, she leapt forward.

Her left hand snagged the seatbelt of the driver, and she yanked hard, making the locking mechanism engage while also remove all slack. The driver was effectively pinned against the seat.

In the same motion she gripped her grandfather's pocket knife and jabbed it into the neck of the man who had grabbed her.

Both men shouted what she could only assume were expletives in Russian, but she was already in motion for the next part of her plan. The driver had hit the brakes, which threw everyone forward. With his seatbelt locked this only served to further incapacitate him, but the other man was thrown forward at an angle as he gripped his injured neck.

Alex went forward as well, reaching for the passenger's weapon, which he'd kept pressed against his left leg. He'd released it to reach up to his injury, and Alex was able to snag it with a quick plunge under his elbow. She brought it up from where she was, leaned over the center console, and took quick aim at the driver.

She pulled the trigger.

Even with a silencer, the noise was frightening in the confines of the car. But she'd been prepared for that. She was no stranger to guns, having been raised around them and later taking concealed weapons training. She owned a couple of 9mm pistols and a hunting rifle she'd inherited from her grandfather. She went to the firing range regularly.

But she'd never fired at another human being.

There was a strange, crushing feeling in her guts, now that she'd done so. Something, she knew, she'd be dealing with later. Maybe for a lot of laters.

For now...

She rolled and did it again, shooting the man she had injured with the knife.

Both men slumped, dead, held upright only by the seatbelts. Blood caked and oozed over both car door windows, the dash, the windshield.

The car was moving again, still in gear and with no pressure on the brake. She quickly searched the man in the passenger's seat and found her phone, and then opened the door and hopped out onto the pavement, the car moving away from her at a slow roll.

In the last second she tossed the handgun back into the car, hoping she'd never have to need one again.

There would be prints. She would be identified. But there would also be a severed zip tie in the back floorboard, and a knife wound in the passenger's neck. Explaining all those details would be an interesting exercise in police investigation.

She didn't intend to be around to witness any of it.

She ran, and when she found a place where she felt she could hide for a moment she slumped against the wall and breathed fast and heavy for a few moments.

Then she doubled at the waist and threw up all over the ground.

Hunched over, hands on her knees, she saw the blood on her hands. It must have come from the man she'd stabbed. Or possibly from the gunshots, she couldn't be sure. There had been a lot of blood, she could now recall. More blood than she would have thought possible. TV and movies hadn't prepared her for the pure gore of the scene.

She retched again.

In her hand was the pocket knife. She carefully wiped its blade on the inside of her tailored coat, folded it closed and put it back in her pocket. She wiped her hands inside the coat as well. It would help conceal some of it, at least. The stain of it was still on her skin, and she wanted nothing more than to find a place to wash. And maybe vomit again.

She assessed her surroundings.

She was several blocks from the Populus offices, but that was one of the last places she intended to go.

Adrian had set up a meeting with the Russians there, and after things went wrong, there was bound to be some chaos and fallout to contend with.

Alex had locked all the building's automated systems with QuIEK, which would have triggered a few outside systems to react. The firm they contracted for security would be there at some point. There might even be a visit from the fire department and police, though Alex had set up an automated alert to tell them this was only a test. She didn't want to pull emergency services away from real problems.

Though, now that she thought about it, this had become more of a real problem than she'd anticipated.

What should she do?

She looked at her phone. It might be one of the most secure devices on the planet, thanks to QuIEK, but she hadn't yet set it up to mask her location when it pinged local towers. She really hadn't intended to, since she used features that made that kind of thing useful. Until now, she hadn't had any reason to stay off of anyone's radar.

But that had just changed in a big way.

She took out the Swiss Army knife again and removed the toothpick. She used this to pop open the SIM card slot on the phone and then removed the tiny chip. She'd keep it for now. She might end up needing it, for one reason or another. She wedged it between the blade and the outer casing of the knife, to keep track of it for later.

Looking around, she spotted a bodega just down the block.

She entered and glanced around. There were security cameras, but otherwise only one lone twenty-something sat bored and slumped at the counter. He was reading a magazine, and Latino music was playing from a beat up radio behind him.

"I need one of those prepaid SIMs," Alex said to him, nodding to the cards hanging behind the counter.

She was careful to keep her hands in her pockets, hiding the bloodstains. The kid, bored and disaffected, reached back and grabbed one of the cards, putting it on the counter. "Anything else?" he asked.

"I called earlier," Alex said. "The owner is holding a package for me in the back. Some things I special ordered."

The kid looked confused. "You talked to Mateo?"

"Right," Alex said, smiling. "He said it would be in a box tied with twine. Brown paper wrapping. It will say 'Sophia' on it somewhere. I ordered it from him a few days ago and he said it was here."

The kid blinked, then shrugged and went to the back to find Sophia's package.

Alex left with the SIM card in her pocket.

She'd make it right, later. But for the moment, the only means she had to pay for anything was her credit cards or the touchless pay system from her phone—disabled, after removing the SIM card. She wanted to avoid triggering any alerts on her accounts, tipping anyone off to where she was.

She made a note of the name and address of the bodega, and of the manager's name—Mateo. She'd send cash and a note. It was the best she could do.

Back out on the street she hurried, but didn't run. She couldn't know if anyone was already out looking for her, so she kept to the fringe of crowds as often as possible. Soon she came to a hotel, modestly upscale, and the type that made a large portion of its income by hosting conventions.

This meant that people were coming in and out constantly, barely recognizable or even noticeable to the staff or anyone else.

Good cover.

She slipped into the restroom just off of the lobby and quickly washed her hands in the crystal basin, watching a stream of crimson run in rivulets into the drain. Another woman came in just as Alex was finishing.

"Are you ok?" the woman asked, studying the carnage in the sink.

Alex smiled. "My wine glass shattered! Can you believe that? I really hate making trouble for people, but you can bet I'm going to have a chat with the manager!"

"Oh!" the woman replied. "Were you hurt badly?"

"Just a small cut," Alex said, cradling her fingers as if to protect the injury. "But it just bled like crazy!" She took two tissues from the dispenser beside the sink and held those to the imaginary cut. "I'm sure they have someone on staff who can look at this."

The woman nodded, and Alex left the restroom.

She was still a mess, and if anyone looked closely, there could be questions. For the moment, however, she'd keep a low profile, and hope no one noticed.

Right now, she needed information.

In the lobby, near the check-in desk, there was a row of computers, meant for guests to use for quick internet access. These, Alex knew, were often unlocked and open to the public. They might be monitored, but she wasn't overly concerned about that right now. She made her way to one of the computers and logged in.

There was a lot that Alex needed to know, but sitting here, near the check-in, was not about surfing the web. She'd have to get to that later.

Right now, what she needed most was cover—an excuse to be within earshot.

She needed a minute to assess things, and a way to camouflage herself so she could leave this hotel and get moving.

She also needed a way to get out of these clothes and get cleaned up, beyond the level achievable in a public restroom.

She sat at the computer, occasionally pretending to be reading something from the screen, and waited.

It took a bit of time, but eventually someone checked in within ear shot. He was a young executive in town for one of the conferences being hosted by the hotel. "Jared Patterson," he said, when asked his name. They told him his room was 846, and handed him two plastic key cards.

Alex waited a beat, and then followed Jared Patterson, slipping in beside him as he stepped into the elevator to the eight floor. When they left the elevator, she took a right as he took a left, but in a moment she turned and followed him from a distance. She watched as he slipped the card into his door, then dragged his suitcase inside.

Alex waited near the elevator bays, watching. It was maybe thirty minutes later when Jared stepped back out into the hall. She turned, hit the down button, and boarded the elevator before he could get there. She rode down along, and then waited in the lobby, watching as Jared exited the elevator and made his way to a registration table in the conference area, checking in whatever event had brought him here.

Alex went to the front desk.

"May I help you?" The girl behind the desk was young, maybe in her early twenties, but smartly dressed. She exuded both confidence and happiness in her work. Friendly.

Alex liked her immediately.

"Hi," Alex smiled, making herself look sheepish. "My husband and I arrived about half an hour ago. I went to look at the spa while he got ready for his conference. But I forgot to take a key card with me! And now he's in there," she waved vaguely at the conference center, "and I probably won't see him again for hours."

The girl smiled and nodded, as if this happened all the time. "No problem, Mrs.?"

"Patterson. The room is registered under my husband's name, Jared Patterson. Room 846."

"Do you have an ID?" the girl asked.

"It's in the room," Alex said, making an embarrassed face. "Honestly, all I wanted was a hot stone massage and a glass of wine after that flight." She rolled her eyes, making an exasperated expression and then laughing at herself, depreciating.

The girl laughed lightly. "No problem Mrs. Patterson, I can get you a new card."

She tapped at her console, and after a moment she handed Alex a card in a paper sleeve. "Enjoy your stay! And definitely get that massage. It's one of the most relaxing things we offer!"

"Oh, believe me," Alex said. "I will!"

She left the front desk and hurried to the elevator, then rode to the eighth floor, making her way quickly to room 846. She held the card against the reader and watched as a little green light flicked on. She heard the *click* of the lock, and she was in.

The room was just like every other hotel room she'd ever seen, with the restroom just off of the entry, a television on the dresser, and a desk and chair close to the window. Jared Patterson's suitcase was on the bed, opened and hastily sifted through to retrieve whatever it was he needed.

Alex rummaged through it herself, retrieving articles of clothing that might come in handy. She also found his laptop, which would *definitely* come in handy. She set this up on the desk.

She then stripped.

She wanted to make this quick, not knowing for certain when Jared might decide to come back. She figured he'd be preoccupied with the conference for at least a couple of hours, and that should be enough time.

She took a quick shower, scrubbing herself clean. She kept her hair dry, not certain she'd have time to blow dry it. But the shower got the blood off her and made her feel fresh and energized again. It helped in psychological ways, as much as physically.

She toweled off, then pulled on some of Jared's clothes. She'd picked the more casual things—jeans and a T-shirt, a pair of sneakers. She could work with these. They weren't all that flattering on her, but they were better by vast degrees from what she'd been wearing earlier. Not just because they were clean from blood—they also changed her *look*.

That was going to be important.

She pulled her hair into a ponytail and tied it with a strip of cloth cut from her blouse. The lacy fringe of it made it look like a fancy hair band. It should—the blouse had cost three hundred dollars.

No regrets. Alex had always felt a little bad about spending so much on clothes, anyway. A vice, and one she'd justified by reminding herself that she was the CEO and Founder of a multi-billion-dollar tech company. One must look the part, mustn't one?

She inspected herself in the full-length mirror across from the bathroom and nodded.

It would do.

She bundled up all of her things, shoving them into the plastic dry cleaning bag from the closet. She'd ditch these somewhere else. She was going to create enough of a stir when Mr. Patterson returned to find someone had been in his room. She wanted to try to keep confirmation that she was that someone as quiet as she could manage, for as long as possible.

At any rate, her immediate physical needs were met. Now she needed information.

She opened Jared's laptop and then went searching for a charging cable in his bag. She found it—thankfully a match for her own phone—and plugged her phone into the laptop. She hadn't yet set up the SIM card, but she didn't need it right now.

The local version of QuIEK was still in memory on the phone, and she used this to crack his laptop's password.

She hit the news sites again, started searching everywhere for information about Populus, Adrian, the Russians.

No mention of Russian operatives, of course, but Adrian and Populus were now getting lots of press.

So was she.

According to nearly every news site, Adrian was dead. He'd been found shot in his office at Populus.

Alex was reeling from that news, but it got worse.

Authorities were looking for *her* as the prime suspect.

They were also looking for her in connection to potential espionage and treason.

She closed the laptop and leaned back in the office chair.

She was breathing heavy, her heart pounding. She'd thought she was in danger before, with the Russians. Now she knew there was so much more.

She was screwed beyond her wildest imagination.

She was on the run now.

CHAPTER FOUR

NOW | ORLANDO, Florida

UCONIC PROSTHETIC TECHNOLOGIES got a lot of good press. It only took Alex fifteen minutes of searching to get a complete profile on the company, from its founders to its current board, and all of its publicly known contracts and relationships. It took only a few minutes more to look at the company through the lens of various government and military databases, to learn a few off-the-books details.

The company had been founded in 1998 under a different name, with a different objective. At that time, it was a Dot-Com aimed at creating a sort of GPS workaround, essentially user-based data gathering to provide customers with custom maps they could print and carry with them, guiding them to hot spots in major cities worldwide. The service would let users customize their trips and share their discoveries with others through the site. It was crowdsourcing before anyone really had a name for it.

But in that pre-smartphone age, the idea couldn't quite gain purchase. Users had to log in from their computers to update the site and provide feedback, and at the time laptops with mobile internet access were still bulky and expensive, and not a common item to take on vacation. Users also had to print out maps, which made them obvious tourists, with side effects such as making them targets for muggers and pickpockets. And if anything was updated on their maps, they'd have to be reprinted, which was often impossible while traveling.

Like many Dot-Coms, the business gained huge investments upfront despite having very little product to show for it.

Unlike most Dot-Coms, however, when the bubble burst and the majority of startups went under, the business managed to pivot and redefine itself.

The problems, including the flaws in the business plan, hadn't escaped the notice of the company's founders, even while the money was easy and free-flowing. Surprisingly, they managed to recognize that they were headed toward an inevitable meltdown. Money from angel investors was good—but if they couldn't build a customer base, things were bound to go pear-shaped at some point.

To solve this, the company had done the unthinkable—they had shifted into a new business model, and invested in a *hardware division* during the rise of the purely digital age.

Showing a shocking level of prescience, they had decided that technology had not yet caught up to their needs. So, if the Mohamed wouldn't go to the mountain... they would *build* technology that served their purpose.

Their first product was the Uconic personal GPS—a wearable technology that resembled a very large wrist watch, which provided rudimentary location data based on pinging cellular towers. It used text-based, turn-by-turn directions to get users from location to location.

It was far from the sleek, tiny, futuristic smartwatches sold in the modern digital age. It was clunky and heavy, and had a severe battery life issue. It also had a tendency to heat up during use, making it uncomfortable to wear for long periods.

But it was the future. It created a buzz. Everyone—everyone who knew it existed, at least—wanted one.

When the dot-com bubble burst, the founders had looked for a way to appease their investors and keep them onboard. They thought they could ride the turmoil, believing it had to level off at some point and dot-coms would be back. *Just wait. Just be patient. Just hold out.*

They were right, as far as it went. Though the digital side of their business might never be relevant again, the hardware side became something of great interest.

Wearable technology was coming into the fore. People wanted better integration with the online world. They wanted to carry it with them, to interact with it in a more organic way. Their first wearable tech—bulky, uncomfortable, ugly—might not have started a revolution, but it did provide some *direction.*

It was the direction of the entire industry, as it turned out. Steve Jobs and Apple eventually took mobile technology to a new level with the introduction of the iPhone, and all the iTechnology that followed. Other companies—from Sony to Samsung to startups most people never heard about—followed suit.

Uconic, on the other hand, took a slightly different path.

The wearable tech was only the start. What would be the *next* step in the interaction of humans with technology?

The answer, as Uconic's leadership considered it, was *integration.*

Once again, the company pivoted, turning their resources toward the development of integrated tech. Cybernetics, prosthetics, human-interface technology—Uconic was determined to be on the cutting edge of all of it.

It got noticed.

Military contracts started to come in, and Uconic began creating technology that helped soldiers navigate the battlefield, communicate with their fellows and commanders, and signal for rescue. These contracts allowed Uconic's leadership to pitch even more *out there* ideas. It gave them a stage from which they could start pushing for advancements that would be more than the next "iPhone killer." Uconic was poised to own a segment of the technology sector that had very little competition and had seen very few advancements.

And the key to it all was that their technology *worked*.

It worked so well, in fact, that when the military became interested in prosthetics, Uconic was among the first companies they approached.

At the same time, advances in medical technology opened the door for Uconic to land contracts in the private sector, and the research and development began to overlap in interesting and remarkable ways.

In 2016 Uconic announced the integration of sophisticated 3D printing technology, coupled with new and cutting edge surgical techniques and next-level implants. They unveiled their work in AI, and the carbon-nanotube neural arrays that effectively allowed them to create a "miniature brain" that could run their tech, and grow alongside the user.

These advancements were recognized for what they were— evolutionary steps forward. Funding poured in. Research and development accelerated. A new era of prosthetics was ushered in.

The result was the Uconic Unity Prosthetic 8, or UUP8.

It was, by all accounts, the most advanced prosthetic on the planet, and it was the arm that Abbey Cooper had been invited to test, after Uconic received more than a million dollars from crowdfunding.

How could they possibly turn Abbey away?

The publicity was worth more than the money, to be frank. Both would be very handy in accelerating development for a technology that could—and probably *would*—change the direction of human and technological evolution.

The opportunity was simply too good to pass up.

There were three UUP8 prosthetics on the planet, Alex discovered. Abbey's was not the first.

One had been given to a wounded soldier, who used it to shake the hand of the President while receiving a Medal of Honor.

The second had been given to a United States Senator who had lost his right arm in combat, years earlier.

The third arm, of course, had been given to Abbey Cooper.

All three were technically on loan. The technology was proprietary and, in some ways, classified. The fact that the recipients would wear it out in the real world, away from scrutiny and supervision, was something of a miracle. It was a sign that somewhere, deeper in the core of the company and its contracts, a more advanced version was already being manufactured.

Alex confirmed this.

Uconic Unity Prosthetic X, the tenth generation, was already in use with the military. It was more than a step beyond the UUP8. It was an evolutionary leap. And as the UUP8 provided more and more user data, the UUPX benefited in myriad ways. Every trial of the civilian system added to and improved the classified system.

It didn't take long for Alex to come to a conclusion, then.

Whoever stole Abbey's arm was after the UUPX technology.

This was all interesting, and it opened a lot of potential windows into what had happened, but it hadn't moved Alex any closer to finding the arm or who had stolen it.

She'd been at this for two days, digging and compiling and digging some more. She now knew more about Uconic and the UUP tech than was likely known by any other single human being in the world, and it wasn't getting her any closer to solving this.

She hated this part.

As long as things were firmly in the digital data realm, Alex could operate entirely off the radar. But there were times—and it was clear this was one of them—that the data stopped telling her any secrets and started telling her that it was time to suit up. She would have to step out of the comfort and relative security of her hiding place and go out into the real world, among the three-dimensional people.

She would have to risk exposure again.

It came to this, sometimes. It was part of the gig. Her dedication and commitment were tested. Her rule was that she never left a job unfinished. That rule couldn't ever be broken. It was the core of all of this.

The client was stuck, trapped in whatever the problem was. She had to solve the problem for them to be free, and that was the only way.

If she walked on a job, she was failing the helpless. She was letting an injustice go unchallenged.

That couldn't happen. Ever.

So it was back out into the heat and humidity of Orlando. Back out to where the odds of being spotted went up, to where the risk of being captured increased.

The good news was that out here, in the big scary world, was also where all the resources were.

You have everything you need, right in front of you.

Her grandfather's voice, always there. Always teaching her. Always giving advice.

The trouble was, the advice only worked if you were actually willing to face the world, to play on this game board and by its rules.

She dressed like a tourist.

The art of urban camouflage was to look like what everyone around you expected you to look like. In Orlando, home to the world's most famous amusement park, that meant Disney-themed clothing. Disney T-shirts, Disney ball caps, Minnie Mouse ears, Disney sunglasses.

She'd snagged all of these on her first day in Orlando, paying cash for everything at the World of Disney store in Disney Springs. She'd even popped for a lanyard ladened with dozens of Disney pins, posing as one of the rabid collectors who raced from swap to swap in the parks. To anyone looking at her, she'd appear to be a soccer mom on vacation, taking a break from the kids, who must be with their dad. All she had to do was smile and be excited, and that was easy enough.

It *was* Disney, after all.

The Disney bubble extended through all of Orlando, and so it worked as well elsewhere as it did on the Disney properties themselves. No one gave her a second look as she walked the sidewalks of downtown Orlando and skirted by the home offices of Uconic Prosthetic Technologies. She had her smartphone mounted on a selfie stick, and chattered away about the "off the beaten path" fun to be found in Orlando, as if talking to a YouTube audience.

This allowed her to take several photos and a great deal of video of a highly secure building with military-grade security.

A few strategically placed "updates" for her audience, as well as some satellite imaging from Google Earth, and she had the whole building mapped out.

Slipping into a coffee shop restroom, she changed into more business-like attire. She shoved everything into the backpack she'd carried in, removed her smart tablet, and then stood on the toilet so she could lift one of the tiles of the suspended ceiling. She shoved the pack as far back in the ceiling as she could and replaced the tile. It might be years before anyone ever found that bag and wondered about it. She might even have some occasion to come back and retrieve it at some point—it was always good to have a stash of clothes in various places.

Emerging from the restroom as a completely different person, Alex ordered an iced latte and took a seat outside, under the shade of an umbrella. It was still oppressively hot here, which had the effect of thinning the surrounding crowd. She could tough it out. The privacy allowed her to openly scan through the images she'd gathered and pull together a virtual map of sorts.

She logged into Smokescreen, picking a bot in Kansas and using that to log into the Orlando public records database. It was easy to find the plans for the Uconic building. More difficult was finding anything that gave her any hint about its security systems.

They were custom. Which should have been expected. This was a technology firm, after all, with government resources that had to be protected. Their systems were encrypted at a level that would have turned back even the world's best hackers.

Alex was no hacker. She had no patience for it. She'd developed QuIEK by sitting down and staying focused and using everything she'd ever learned and everything she was still learning, but it had taken years to brute-force her way through the code.

With QuIEK, however, she virtually walked through

Uconic's systems as if it wasn't there. It was less about hacking and more about being in a sort of god mode on the system.

Uconic's digital security may have been like busting through a wall of tissue paper, but their physical security was impressive. And tight. There were vulnerabilities, though.

People, for one, were always a vulnerability in any security system. These people were highly trained, however, and likely wouldn't fall for any simple tricks. Alex would have to come up with some other way in.

She spotted it and smiled. With all the technology and resources she had at her disposal, it was refreshing to occasionally find that the easiest solutions were the best.

Her only regret was that she'd have to go fish that backpack out of the ceiling after all.

CHAPTER FIVE

———————

THE SECURITY GUARD scanned her ID and then looked from it to her face and back to the screen in front of him.

He smiled and handed her the ID card that she'd only printed a half hour earlier.

She'd barely made it to Uconic in time, only just arriving as the rest of the moms and kids and teachers were filing in from the buses and cars parked out front.

It had taken a bit to get everything pulled together. Creating a fake ID was easy, but she also needed to put her name and credentials into not just Uconic's systems but also into the computers at Levy Elementary School, in Bryan, Texas.

Still relatively easy.

The real time suck, though, was finding a Texas A&M T-shirt in Orlando, on short notice. She'd resorted to paying someone to rush print one on a blank maroon tee. It was passable, and finished off the "mom escort" vibe she was going for. She'd even doubled down, having the printer include "Proud Future Aggie Mom!" on the back.

Once inside Uconic, she joined the rest of the tour, gliding slowly along as their tour guide walked them through various public spaces in the facility.

They were treated to a tour of one of the robotics labs, where a bizarre collection of arms and legs and hands were suspended in mid-air by cables and conduits.

In an effort to make it seem less macabre, someone had placed a number of Disney-themed objects in the room—including a couple of hands wearing fat, white Mickey gloves, waving enthusiastically at the kids.

This did very little to lessen the creep factor.

No one questioned Alex being part of the crowd. She was just one more mom, festooned in local tourist accoutrement, and of course wearing her maroon pride out front, as was customary. She was able to glide along with the tour until she finally spotted the elevator she'd been looking for.

This would be the tricky part, but she'd mentally rehearsed it dozens of times.

As the tour guide took the kids and the escorts to a large auditorium, Alex paused by the elevator, holding her smartphone to the sensor plate.

QuIEK did its work, and the doors slid open.

She stepped inside and leaned against the control panel, staying hidden as the doors closed completely. She then shucked her backpack, unzipping it and removing her more professional clothing.

She quickly changed and then rolled her other clothes and set them aside. She unzipped the backpack entirely, opening it wide and turning it inside out. The interior couldn't have been more of contrast to the outside—shifting the bag from a pink Jansport to a leather Gucci in one quick turn.

She'd paid nearly five hundred dollars for the custom work, and the effect came off seamlessly. Money well spent.

She shoved the clothes into the bottom of the bag. It was only then that she hit the button for the floor she wanted.

She turned, the Gucci bag slung over one arm like a large purse, and took a breath.

Suddenly she noticed her reflection in the polished surface of the elevator doors.

There was a ding, and the doors were sliding open as she hurriedly grabbed the Minnie Mouse ears from her hair, shoving them into the bag just as the doors opened onto the corridor.

She smoothed her hair as she stepped out and walked confidently in the direction of the research offices.

From the pocket of her coat she removed the ID badge she'd printed alongside her Texas ID and slung the lanyard over her neck. It looked identical to the Uconic badges, but lacked the internal chip that would open doors and activate computer systems for her.

That wasn't an issue, however, as long as she had her smartphone.

The real issue was that, in a few seconds, she'd have to surrender the smartphone as she passed through a security checkpoint, and then scan her badge to pass through the gate, in full view of the guard.

It was going to take a bit of timing. And fumbling. Fumbling was very important in this kind of work, Alex had discovered.

She got to the security checkpoint and smiled at the guard, then made a show of struggling to remove the lanyard from around her neck, trying to untangle it from the strap of her purse. "How did I do that?" she said aloud to herself, struggling and then finally dropping the purse to the floor. She stooped to pick it up, just as the guard leaned forward.

"Everything ok?" He asked.

"Oh! Fine, I'm sorry. I think I need coffee."

As she knelt to pick up her purse with one hand, she raised the ID badge with the other, held in the same hand that was also holding her smartphone.

QuIEK opened the door for her, and as she stood she started to walk through the door.

"Ma'am," the guard said.

She stopped, looking at him, an expression of embarrassment and confusion on her face.

"You have to put your purse and phone on the belt," he said, pointing to the conveyor in front of him.

She laughed self consciously. "Right! I'm sorry!" She placed both her bag and the phone on the belt, then pushed through the security door. She passed through a scanner as she entered, and on the other side she picked up her things from the conveyor.

"Have a nice day ma'am," the guard said.

"Thanks. It has to get better, right?"

"So they tell me," the guard smiled.

Alex put her phone in her pocket and once again hung the bag over her arm, then moved past the guard station and into the research wing of Uconic Prosthetics.

These were offices used by not only Uconic's on-staff researchers, but also by visiting researchers and other VIPs. Strangers moved through the facility on a regular basis, either coming in as representatives of the military or government, or as investors or partners. Alex had counted on this to help keep her anonymity in check.

But that didn't change the fact that she was currently in the belly of the beast—a known fugitive being hunted by every government agency with a string of letters in its name, and she was smack in the middle of a technology business with ties to those same agencies.

It was a very dangerous game to play.

And for all Alex knew, the risk might not pay off. She might find nothing here that was any more of a lead than what she'd found simply by breaking into their servers. But it was all she had to go on for the moment. The hope was to find something that would give her some kind of direction.

The offices in this wing were largely first-come-first-serve. They weren't meant to be permanent spaces, since most of the people using them were only here temporarily. They were simply meant to be a private space for visitors to do a bit of work and make some phone calls.

As such, the entire space had a very impermanent and stark feel. The computers were uniform and nondescript. There was no art on the walls. No personal items on the desks. Alex had worked from places like this as she'd built Populus and had vowed that her own business would be much more personable. Populus had visiting offices as well, but Alex had made sure that each space had an organic and welcoming feel—artwork, plants, little touches that made it comfortable enough for someone to spend their time without feeling as if their soul were being sucked out by the fluorescent lights over their heads.

Drab spaces aside, however, Alex admired Uconic for its advanced systems architecture, as well as its public mission. The technology here really was remarkable—the sharpest apex of cutting edge. And if their publicity were even partially on point, the company was out to restore mobility and personal autonomy to people who needed it most. The disabled and the injured all had reason to admire the company.

Alex tried not to judge them by their government contracts. She knew all too well how easy it was to become beholden to a powerful entity that had different plans for the technology you were building.

She found a cubicle that instinctively felt like the least desirable space in the room. It was oriented so that it had not even the slightest view of a window. It opened to an interior wall, and one of the furthest from either the restrooms or the little break room, where coffee and snacks would be. It was also the furthest from the wing's entry and exit.

It was, however, closest to the stairs.

An alarm would sound the second someone used the door, but Alex liked to keep at least one exit nearby, in case she needed to evacuate in a hurry. Which did happen, occasionally.

This was also one of the more private cubicles, however. No one passed behind it, and no one was likely to decide to use it. Alex stashed her bag in the back corner of the cubicle, under the desk, intending to leave it there when she made her exit. She felt a twinge of regret at losing the custom bag, but she could get another one made, if she needed it. It was easier to leave things behind.

A lesson she seemed to be perpetually reinforcing in her life.

She slipped the fake ID she'd made out of the bag and put it into the inner pocket of her coat. She then took a seat and used QuIEK to unlock the computer in front of her.

It was actually more of a dummy terminal than a full-blown computer. It had a CPU and some limited storage, but it linked to a virtual operating system on the Uconic servers.

Alex had already had this experience, logging in virtually from off site and exploring every crevice of the system, looking for anything that might help her client. Now she logged on to create a distraction.

Uconic's cyber security included key logging for every terminal in the building. These were buffered locally and uploaded to a database each hour, tagged with the ID of the terminal that generated them. Alex hadn't had to worry about key logging when she'd broken in remotely, but now every stroke on the keyboard would be recorded, unless she disabled it.

She did this, easy enough.

What she needed now were the keystrokes of every other user on the network. She also needed to decrease the buffer and the reporting interval. She modified the system's governing protocols so that every keystroke on every terminal in the building was going straight from the buffer to the logging database, all at once.

The system would see this as a DoS or "denial of service" attack.

Hackers sometimes shut down websites or servers by flooding them with inputs or requests, essentially gumming up the pipes and preventing anyone else from using the system. It was the kind of attack that was typically only used to block user access, but Alex had another idea in mind.

An alarm chirped from the overhead speakers, and an automated voice announced, "Please stand away from your systems. We are experiencing a security breech. Please stand away from your systems."

Alex, dutifully, stood away from her system, as did everyone else on the floor.

They shuffled away from the computers and started congregating out on the floor, chatting and asking each other if anyone knew what was going on.

Alex, like so many others, was checking her phone.

Unlike anyone else, she was logged into Smokescreen, using a bot in Vermont to tip the final domino.

With a few quick taps, and running a pre-built protocol, she found the automated systems for the building, including the elevator controls, and shut these down.

More alarms, more automated announcements, and this time the security guard from up front came into the space and ordered them to get to the stairs and make their way down to the lobby.

There were grumbles and complaints, protests that this was probably just a bug, that their coffee would get cold, that they should at least be allowed to grab their personal belongings. Not everyone dutifully filed toward the door.

Alex, being the closest, was there first.

She pushed through, letting the alarm sound, and the door closed behind her.

She'd only have a few seconds before someone else came through, and she didn't waste any time. She sprinted up the stairs and rounded the corner, barely making it to the next flight as people started pushing through the door and starting their descent.

For several long minutes, Alex waited. The sound echoed up to her as people plodded, loudly, down the steps, chatting in excited tones as they went. Eventually the sound started to fade until finally everyone filed out of the ground floor doors.

The next phase was going to be tricky, especially if there happened to be a number of executives coming down this stairway.

In her planning, however, Alex had noted that this stairwell was one of three, and that the Executive offices were closest to one on the opposite side of the building. During an emergency, the higher ups would have a more or less private exit, and this one should stay empty from the research floor up.

That was the best laid plan, anyway.

And of course...

The man emerged from above her, dressed in a very expensive suit and tie, and looking exactly like his photos from the news stories and the company website that Alex had studied during her research.

Roderick Verice. The CEO of Uconic Prosthetic Technologies.

He stopped when he saw her, his expression becoming perplexed but stern.

"You're going the wrong way," he said.

ALEX FROZE, and the two of them waited, looking each other over.

"You're not supposed to be here, are you?" Verice said.

She closed her eyes slowly and tilted her chin down. "No," she said. "I just... I thought everyone would be downstairs for this fire drill or whatever it is, and I... wanted to see."

"To see what?" Verice asked.

She looked upstairs, an expression of longing on her face. "The top," she said quietly. Then looked at him, "I'm just a consultant, Mr. Verice. I don't even really work here. But one day..."

He had been studying her, and now his expression changed, softened. "You want to be an executive some day? Maybe a CEO?" He was smiling at her, and it was sympathetic and understanding.

"I know I'm supposed to be in the lobby, with everyone else," she said. "But I just thought this might be a chance to stand and take it all in, just for a few seconds. To sort of... I don't know... *visualize* myself in that space."

Verice laughed lightly, and leaned over the stair rails a bit, looking down. The sound of the alarm and the security announcement chirped in periodically, but otherwise all that could be heard was the distant murmur of people in the lobby, echoing up through an open stairwell door.

"I normally would have taken the stairs closer to my office, but I just happened to be on this side. So..." he smiled at her. "Today's your lucky day. Come with me."

He turned and went back up the stairs, with her close behind.

It was three more flights before they made it to the executive floor. "You wouldn't have been able to get in, anyway," he said, holding his badge up and looking back over his shoulder. "Your pass wouldn't give you access to anything above the floor you're cleared for."

"Ah!" she laughed. "I hadn't thought of that." Almost subconsciously she put a hand on the bulge in her pocket, where her mobile phone rested.

He chuckled, and as they came to the door, he pressed his badge to the reader. There was a beep and a click, and he took hold of the door, opening it for her.

She stepped through with a smile and a nod, and once on the other side she stood as if overwhelmed by everything she was seeing, turning slowly to take it all in.

She spotted the office she needed to access.

"Not quite as impressive as you might have imagined, I'm sure," Verice said, chuckling. "Just an office space, in the end. Though we do have slightly higher-grade furnishings, I'll admit."

She turned to him, smiling. "It's wonderful," she said. "I can't tell you how much I appreciate you letting me see it."

He nodded. "I'm... sorry, I don't actually know your name."

"Karen Addison," she said. "I'm a consultant, here from Passive LTI."

"The medical technologies firm," he nodded. "I thought we usually had Tim Isaacs visiting."

"You do," Alex nodded. "I tagged along, trying to learn more about the account and help out with some of the workload. I was brought on a couple of months ago."

Verice nodded, accepting this.

Alex saw some telltale signs, though, that he might not be buying it completely. He'd check in on Karen Addison after this conversation finished.

And he'd find that her story held up. There was even a photo of her on the company profile page. If he happened to dig further, he'd even find her office extension, and hear her voice greet him if he called.

Alex had built profiles like these at hundreds of companies worldwide, complete with official email addresses and phone numbers. She was a ghost employee at some of the biggest companies in the world. It came in handy.

"Well, even the CEO is required to vacate during a security breech," he said, holding the door open for her.

She nodded. She was so close, but with Verice watching her she stood no chance of getting into that office. She would only need a few minutes.

"I... know that we're already kind of breaking the rules," she said. "But I heard..."

"What?" Verice asked, curious.

"I heard you could see Disney World from this building." She made a face and looked down, embarrassed.

Verice laughed, a sharp bark. "You're kidding!"

She covered her eyes with a hand, cringing. "I know! I'm sorry, I just... well, I've never been, and I may not get a chance on this trip. I'm kind of a Disney nerd. I've always wanted to go, and to be *this close*..."

He was laughing lightly, and looking around, conspiratorially. "Don't tell anyone I said this," he whispered, "but I'm a bit of a 'Disney nerd' myself. Follow me."

He led her to the door of the very office she was trying to enter and used his ID card to open the door. He motioned her inside. "Take a look. It'll have to be quick, but you won't be disappointed."

She had her phone out, hidden in her palm and pressed against her leg as she stepped to the large windows overlooking Orlando. Sure enough, she spotted Disney World in the distance.

She had to admit, there really was something a bit magical about seeing a fairytale castle rising from the landscape, just beyond the modern buildings and billboards and busy streets.

"Oh, wow!" she gushed, holding her phone up and moving from horizon to horizon of the corner office. She turned back to him, her expression almost tearful. "I'm so grateful, Mr. Verice."

He smiled at her, then nodded. "Alright, time to go."

They left the office then, and took the stairs. They chatted on their way to the ground floor, and as they exited into the bedlam of people milling about in the lobby, awaiting further orders from security, Verice excused himself to go speak with the head of security.

Alex made her way calmly to an exit she had prepared in advance, having disabled the security on the door with a quick assist from QuIEK. In moments, she'd made her way out of the building and into the bright, hot, ridiculously humid Orlando day.

No one even noticed she'd left.

CHAPTER SIX

THE CAMERA on her phone could record in 360 degrees, which allowed her to not only capture every detail of the Orlando landscape leading to Disney, but the interior of the office as well.

She would have preferred unfettered and unmonitored access to the space, and a chance to physically search it, but a 3D scan of the place, alongside all the digitally retrievable information she'd gathered, might give her everything she needed.

This had been a huge gamble, but she'd learned quite a bit about Uconic, and its CEO. Top of that list was that Roderick Verice seemed to be a very good man.

She'd studied everything she could find about him before going in, and other than a few trolling comments about him in social media and the odd blog post, nearly everyone who had ever had contact with him came away with the same impression. He was one of the good guys, and he was determined to do a lot of good with his company as well.

That was comforting. It made things a little easier. It didn't entirely eliminate Uconic in perhaps playing a role in the theft of Abbey's prosthetic arm, but Alex believed that businesses reflected the ideology and temperament of their leadership. Verice was a good man, so his company was more likely to be a good company.

She had uploaded the 360 scan of the office to the cloud via one of her bots. The account was completely off the books and untraceable, thanks to QuIEK. It also had unlimited storage and was accessible via a number of virtual operating systems running the software Alex needed.

She was putting this to work now. Using 3D modeling software, she was able to create a virtual version of the office she'd been standing in with Verice. This included the scans taken as she'd entered and exited the office, holding her phone at a few different angles and elevations as she passed through. With the multi-lens camera recording in 4K, she had made away with some remarkably detailed shots of the place. And with 3D extrapolation, the virtual version of the space was just about as complete as it could get.

The important bits, at least, were captured in detail.

The room was less of an office and more of a joint space where the executives could meet to look over prototypes and discuss strategies and plans. There were a number of tables set up in the room, and book cases and display cabinets lined the walls. It was a library of sorts, with everything oriented toward Uconic's line of research and development. There were even working models of some of their prosthetics, the occasional photo rendering of a 3D model, blueprints and schematics, and reams and tomes of related data, printed for quick reference and placed in easy-to-identify binders.

What Alex was looking for, however, was stamped on the outsides of these binders, as well as on various papers and items spread on table surfaces in the office.

Almost everything about Uconic was kept in its various databases, but there was one set of information that Alex hadn't been able to uncover. Which meant that it was either entirely kept on physical medium, or more likely was kept on systems that were not part of the general network. There were hints and footprints, bits of data that pointed her to the conclusion that everything she needed was in this secured office on the executive floor. And as she moved through the virtual space, that conclusion was confirmed.

Stamped on the binders, on blueprints and schematics, and sometimes on the 3D models and prototypes themselves, were the names of Uconic's various partners and customers. Many of these were off-the-record clients—entities with a strong interest in Uconic research and development, who preferred to keep that interest a secret. This included various government agencies, not just in the US but worldwide, as well as private-sector companies that played on the world stage.

She noted all of these. Any one of them could provide a lead. But there were far more than Alex had expected, and it became obvious that it would take months, maybe years to parse through everything. She would need a way to narrow things down.

Her virtual snoop session complete, Alex saved the 3D rendering and logged out. She leaned back against the stack of pillows on her bed, staring at the tablet on her lap.

She felt tired.

For two years now she'd been doing this. Running from city to city, finding someone who needed her help, and then pouring all of her energy into solving their problem. It felt good. It gave her a purpose.

But what about her own problem?

Her fingers hovered over the icon she'd put on the home screen. It was a single-click app that would aggregate all the information she'd need. It would automatically ping several random bots on Smokescreen, have them pull files and data from databases all over the world—public, private, and top secret. She could have a full report on how the search for her was going and know every move that every US agency was making.

A progress report that let her stay several steps ahead.

But she couldn't face it right now. She was tired. She needed a break.

She was staying at an Airbnb, paid for with a prepaid credit card using one of hundreds of accounts she'd created, with false user profiles that placed her home in dozens of cities across the country. She'd be shocked if anyone even thought to try to trace this part of Smokescreen, but even if they did, it would take thousands of man hours just to get a start on tracking her accounts.

So she was safe. She was confident of that. Believing it was the only thing that allowed her to sleep at night.

This Airbnb was comfortable, cozy, and private. The owners had given her an access code and some instructions, all via email. She'd never even met them. She had the whole house to herself, and her pick of bedrooms. She chose the one with windows overlooking the lake.

It was still early. She was tired, but maybe she should take a walk. Get some fresh air.

Be *Alex Kayne*—for just a little bit.

She changed into running clothes and pulled on a pair of sneakers, then slipped out of the back door of the house. There was a wooded jogging path that ran through here, just beyond the property line.

If she went right she'd be moving along the lake's edge. If she went left she'd cut through the woods, emerging further along a stream that terminated at the lake. There was a bridge there that Alex found kind of charming, and so she'd defaulted to that direction for the past few mornings.

She turned left, trotting at a slow but steady pace, letting her muscles loosen and the tension ease before starting to ramp up speed.

Eventually she was in a solid run, the wind blowing the perspiration from her face, her lungs and legs pumping. There were more people on the path than she typically saw when she ran in the mornings. Only the dedicated ran at 5 AM, she supposed. She'd been in the habit for so long now that it didn't phase her.

Keeping fit was part of her survival strategy.

She rounded a bend in the path, and up ahead was the bridge. That was her designated cool-off point, a place where she'd stop for some water and a breather, where she could lean on the bridge railing and look out over the stream and the lake beyond. A narrow tunnel of trees and foliage made the site look like something out of a fantasy novel, and she'd found that she adored it.

She'd remember this place, if and when she ever returned to the area. She would never rent the same Airbnb again, of course. Never go back. But the path was public, and she could blend in here easy enough. She could come back here to enjoy the view, someday.

A group of over-60 runners stomped by on the wooden slats of the bridge, breaking her out of her reverie. She watched them go by and then fade into the distance, a group of friends united by their interest in running. She envied them.

Two years on the run, and the thing that wearied her most was this. Being alone like this. Watching others live lives she might never have the chance to experience.

She yearned for friendships like that. She ached to have someone she could fully confide in. But to everyone she ever knew—friend, family, or foe—she was a ghost. A girl on the run. A fugitive being hunted.

Contacting anyone she knew would only end up disrupting their lives.

There was a park near the bridge, and she could see families out enjoying the day. A mother patiently trailed her toddler daughter at the top of a set of steps. An Asian couple helped their little boy, cartoon backpack on his back, as he leapt from a small set of boulders into the grass, then raced to the edge of a fountain. Other couples, other families, other groups of friends milled about in the park, simply enjoying an unassuming, uninterrupted life.

In small ways, Alex could be a part of all of it. She could watch and observe, listen in on conversations and imagine her side of it, if she could participate. She could stand or sit close by, allowing small family dramas to play out in her presence, so she could pretend to be a part of them.

It was a little sad and pathetic, she knew. A vicarious life. It was all she could have right now. It might be as much as she could ever expect.

A man was jogging up the path she'd used, and Alex saw him see her, then angle toward her. She sighed. He was obviously going to hit on her, which would lead to the inevitable shut down and possibly some awkward moments on the running path, depending on which direction they each chose.

Being hit on wasn't entirely unpleasant, though. She didn't mind, most of the time. It only bothered her that she was leading the guy on. There was zero chance they'd carry a connection any further than this moment, this series of smiles and casual brushes of a hand on an arm, if it even went that far.

She wouldn't have minded connecting further, most of the time, but it was just impossible. Alex Kayne couldn't have a date. It created too many variables. It opened up too many vulnerabilities.

"Hi," the guy said, smiling and pausing. "You mind?" He was motioning to the railing, and Alex nodded.

He huffed and leaned forward, resting his arms on the smooth wood. "Sorry for the sweat. It's really humid here."

She smiled. "I've noticed," she said.

It wasn't the only thing she noticed.

The guy wasn't from here. She'd picked up on this because of what he'd said—*really humid here*—but also because, despite being fit, his skin was a little pale. And he really was sweating profusely. He wasn't acclimated to this climate.

"You're from out of town?" Alex asked, curious despite herself.

He laughed. "Is it that obvious? Yeah. Up north."

She nodded. "I'm from Colorado," she lied. "What has you in Orlando?"

He shook his head, as if he hadn't really intended to talk about it, but said, "I'm doing a little work in the area. It should be over soon," he smiled, then nodded to the lake view beyond the tunnel of trees. "That's a pretty amazing view. Kind of surreal."

Alex nodded, leaning onto the rail and bending her left knee while extending her right leg into a stretch. "Yeah, I've come here for the past several days. Since arriving in town. It's peaceful, you know?"

The guy nodded. "I'm Eric, by the way. Eric Symon." He held out a hand.

"Hi Eric," she said, taking his hand.

The touch lingered.

"And you're Alex Kayne," he said, smiling.

She smiled back, "Yes, that's me, Agent Symon."

He blinked. "Oh... you..."

"Figured it out, yes," Alex said. "I suppose this is where you'll cuff me and the two agents sitting and trying to stay hidden over by the restrooms will escort me to a car somewhere?"

He laughed lightly. "Well, yes, actually. Your file was right. You're pretty smart. It's been awhile, but we finally caught up."

"Can I ask, what did it?"

He reached into the back pockets of his shorts and took out a pair of handcuffs, holding them up as if asking permission. Alex nodded, but he paused before putting them on. He looked around at the families, the children playing all around them. "I'd rather not cause a lot of chaos here. You're caught, you know that, right? It's not just those two agents. There are two more just behind us on this path, two more on the path beyond, and about twenty combing through the Airbnb you rented."

"Got me dead to rights," Alex smiled, nodding. "No scenes."

He nodded. "Good. So as for how we found you, it was really a lucky break. One of our agents is on vacation, taking her kids to Disney World. She spotted you at a coffee shop, of all places. Recognized you right away and called us in. Which was surprising, I have to tell you, because we had tracked you to Iowa or something. You have some kind of VPN set up, we think."

"I pay homeless people to get online and pretend to be me," she said.

He nodded. "Lying. But that's ok."

"It is," Alex said. "Ok, so dumb luck. That's good. I can't plan for everything."

"No," Agent Symon said. "You're smart though. I only know a couple of people who might be as smart as you. One's an archeologist, kind of a modern day Indiana Jones. He does some consulting with the Bureau. But I think you're smarter, really. So it's kind of a kick to bring you in."

She smiled. "Eric, can I just say one thing, before you cuff me and hand me over?"

He looked at her, then shrugged.

"You really shouldn't count your arrests before they're latched."

She grabbed him by the wrist, with one hand taking his forefinger and bending it the wrong way, hard.

He couldn't cry out, the pain and surprise were so sudden, and before he could recover she twisted around, bringing his arm into an awkward position behind him. Then she lifted up hard and sharp.

In the position he was in, he had two choices, and his anatomy was working against him on one of them. He could either stand his ground and let his arm be broken at the elbow, or he could lean forward to keep the sharp and sudden pressure from causing him injury.

Biology and survival instinct won the day, and in an instant Agent Symon was toppled forward, flipped over the bridge rail and into the shallow waters. The current was strong enough that it carried him quickly toward the lake, even as he flapped and struggled to regain control.

Alex sprinted away then, running at top speed, straight into the playground.

People hadn't quite noticed what had happened, and the sight of someone running through on the jogging trail was nothing new. Alex cut away from the trail, however, and ran through the playground.

The two agents she'd spotted by the restrooms broke and raced toward her. They hadn't drawn weapons yet, which was a relief. Not only did it mean they were trying to take her alive, it also prevented any stray shots from hitting innocent bystanders.

There were more agents present than Eric had indicated, however. Two people rose up from benches, dressed in plain clothes and now racing toward her.

They were closing in on her, using the playground equipment to help fence her in. Alex sprinted directly toward the equipment, however, and leapt.

She took hold of a chin-up bar, and used it to launch herself into a high arch, then grasped and snagged the metal hand rail of a spiraling ladder. An agent reached for her, trying to grab her legs, and Alex flipped around, catching the agent around the neck with both her ankles. She rolled, holding to the ladder with one hand and twisting the agent's neck in such a way that he had no choice but to roll with her. He flipped onto the ground, legs flailing, and catching the other agent in the chin.

The two undercovers were getting close, and Alex let go of the ladder, falling to the mulch-covered ground and tucking into a roll at the last second. She hit, rolled forward, and then leapt through a large, circular hole in a piece of the playground equipment.

She found herself in a sort of hamster maze of plastic tubes and slides. One of the undercover agents scurried in through the same hole, and Alex found herself wrestling momentarily with a woman well trained in taking people down.

Alex grabbed the straps of the woman's tank top, twisting them hard until they were strangling the woman. She rolled over her then, just in time for the second undercover agent to poke his head in and reach for her.

Alex made a gap in the tank top straps and wrapped this quickly around the man's hand. She then let go.

The woman's weight carried the man forward. Alex rolled back on her haunches and kicked upward, catching the man in the chin and banging his head against the top of the play structure.

He collapsed, dazed, his full weight on top of the other woman, who was struggling to climb free.

Alex dove out of the structure and sprinted to the restrooms.

There would be more agents, she knew. And she had limited options for escape.

She came to the restrooms, which were made of cinder blocks and natural stone, with stalls that had no doors and polished steel for mirrors. There were no ceiling panels to push open, no back doors, no place to hide. Which was why she didn't bother entering, but instead quickly scaled the side, clutching the natural stone with a rock-climber's grip.

She made her way to the roof, and then kicked over a large, metal cover that looked identical to the other two utility boxes on the roof. She grabbed the backpack she'd stashed there, days earlier, and raced to the edge of the roof. There were three electrical cables extending from poles to the top of the restrooms. Two were supplying power for the restrooms and the park. The other was a fake. She unclamped it, and pulled it free, then gathered it, reducing the slack. She tugged it a couple of times, and then leapt.

There were cheers from the kids, and excited yelling from the people who had been in the park. There may have been cries of "halt!" from any agents who happened to be nearby. But Alex wasn't paying attention to any of this.

She swung through trees, clearing all but the small branches in her path, and when she'd gotten to the right spot she let go.

She was in mid-air for only a few seconds and then landed with a roll in the soft ground of the woods. She sprinted from there, dodging trees and underbrush, and leaping over a small stream that led to the larger one she'd left behind.

The one where she'd dumped Agent Eric Symon.

She burst out of the trees and into the parking lot of a Dairy Queen. Parked beside the dumpster was a beat up Honda Civic. There was an orange parking violation sticker on the driver-side window, but otherwise it looked exactly as it had when she'd left it there, days earlier.

She retrieved the key from under the rock where she'd hidden it, and in moments she and her backpack bug-out kit were on the road and racing away.

The Airbnb was burned—figuratively—along with everything she'd left behind. She took a phone out of the backpack and hit the icon for "Scorched Earth." That would wipe out the electronics she'd left, though there wasn't much anyone would have found on those, anyway.

"Dumb luck," she sneered, shaking her head. "Fantastic."

She took a turn and joined traffic as she merged onto the highway. She'd swap cars in half an hour and hit one of the stashes of cash and credit cards later that night.

She'd have to find a new place to stay, even though staying here, in Orlando, was just about the dumbest move she could make.

The job wasn't finished.

But on the plus side, the FBI would assume she'd leave Orlando at the first opportunity.

She'd have to be crazy to stay.

CHAPTER SEVEN

AGENT ERIC SYMON was soaking wet and as pissed off as he'd ever been. Which was why everyone thought he was nuts when he started laughing, climbing out of the stream with water pouring off of him, and a little scratched up from the stones and branches he'd encountered on his way to the lake.

"She got away, didn't she?" he asked one of the agents who had come to retrieve him.

"She... did," the agent said.

"She's some kind of ninja," Agent Julia Mayher replied.

She was adjusting her tank top, trying not to be obvious about adjusting her bra as well. "I've never seen anyone move like that," Mayher said.

"Parkour," Eric said, shaking his head and wringing water from his T-shirt.

Mayher stared at him.

"X-games? Extreme sports? You don't know what parkour is?"

"There's nothing about that in her file," she replied.

"Obviously the file needs updating," Eric said, shaking his head as he marched up the bank and onto the jogging path.

The other agents, including some from the Airbnb search, were gathered and comparing notes. And in some cases, bruises.

"She couldn't have known we were coming," one of the suited agents said. He was a local, someone Eric didn't know well. "But she was prepared. She had an escape route."

"She probably has more than one," Eric said. "We muffed this."

"How could we know?" Mayher asked.

Eric sighed. "We should have. She's proven to be resourceful. She's a planner. She's managed to stay ahead of us for two years now. So yeah, we should have known she wouldn't be quite as vulnerable as she appeared. But that's where we are. She's in the wind and we're standing here dripping." He swept a hand down his shirt, slinging away some water. "We'll have to regroup. I need to debrief everyone, find out what we know now that we didn't know before."

"We know she's a ninja," Agent Mayher grumbled.

"She's a ghost now," one of the suited agents said. "No way she sticks around Orlando. We should start blocking roads, setting up checkpoints."

"Do that," Eric said. "I'll also have my team stick around and do something that's actually productive."

The agent blinked. "I don't..."

"She's not leaving," Eric said. "She'll stay here until she's finished with whatever brought her here. That's her M.O. She's going to stay in Orlando until whatever she's come here for has run its course. So we need to shift gears, figure out what that job is."

"How do we know her M.O.?" The agent asked. "I've seen her file. She doesn't seem to have any patterns."

Eric shook his head. "She has patterns. They just don't make sense to us, and I think it's because we're not thinking about her in the right light. We keep after her like her only goal is to stay on the run, to evade capture." He shook his head and gratefully accepted a towel that was handed to him. He ran this over his hair and dabbed at his chest, arms, and legs. "I don't think that's it. We've gotten close to her before, and sometimes that has put her on the run. But sometimes she digs in, disappears in the city she's in and then re-emerges there before hitting the road again. She's not going to these cities on a whim, or on the run. She's doing something here. She has a task."

"That's great, Eric," Agent Mayher said. "And it might be helpful, but only if we can figure out what she's doing here."

"Which is exactly what I want us to turn our attention to," Eric said. "We have intel that she infiltrated Uconic Prosthetics? We'll start there."

Everyone nodded, made whatever notes that needed to be made, and debriefed with Eric one by one.

When they were done he dismissed them, sending them to take on various tasks. They would definitely be watching the highways, the flights, the buses. Eric knew that was pointless, but it had to be done. It was CYA.

The real answers would come as they looked closer at her reason for being in Orlando. Eric was sure of that.

What was she looking for at Uconic? What was in that facility that would make Alex Kayne sit still and make mistakes?

Because that's what this was.

She might have planned ahead, might have gotten away, but she'd made a mistake. And that wasn't like her.

Eric had studied everything there was to know about Alex Kayne. He knew her, probably better than any other human being alive.

No family. Not really. One estranged sibling she hadn't spoken to since they were kids. Parents dead. An aunt living in La Grange, Texas, whose husband had died shortly after Alex had gone on the run.

Her company, Populus, had more or less gone down in flames once its two founders were linked to a Russian conspiracy. Alex on the run, Adrian dead. The whole business had been sold off piece by piece until it wasn't much more than a whisper.

What was interesting to Eric, at the moment, were the *new* facts that were emerging.

There was nothing in Alex's file that indicated she was into parkour, for example. She wasn't even known to be much of a jogger, though she'd been jogging every day since they'd tracked her to this location.

She was learning new skills, picking up new habits.

What else had she learned in two years? What other new resources did she have?

And how was she doing all of this alone?

That was another curiosity about her. Eric had been a part of hundreds of manhunts over the years, and one of the keys to tripping someone up and bringing them in was almost always their relationships. Being on the road full time, being estranged from friends and family and locked out of familiar and comfortable relationships, that was rough. It was exhausting and depleting. It tripped people up, eventually.

What most people didn't realize was that humans were almost always dependent on some form of interaction with other humans. And not in the touch-feely psychological way, necessarily. That sort of thing was important, too.

But the reality of life in the modern world was that if you wanted to stay out in the cold, and survive the experience, you needed someone on the *inside*. You needed people who weren't on the run, to help you make arrangements that required you to be "in the system," as it were.

Hotels, car rentals, flights—these were all things that required identification, money, access. Alex Kayne seemed to have money, and she was pretty good at faking identification, but how was she gaining so much access?

For that, she really needed other people. At least, in Symon's experience, that was the case. So the fact that she seemed to be able to sidestep that, to move around freely without needing anyone's help, that was just baffling.

Unless maybe she was a sociopath?

That was something one of the profilers had suggested, and Eric had kept it in his back pocket.

If Alex Kayne *were* a sociopath, it meant she could be completely divorced of what was commonly thought of as human emotions and attachments. Depending on the degree of her sociopathy, she might be just fine on her own for months, maybe even years. She'd have a lack of empathy for others, and would look at them as less than herself, beneath contempt or even recognition.

That didn't gel with the rest of her profile, but Eric couldn't rule it out entirely. Sociopaths could hide in plain sight their whole lives, mimicking the emotions and behaviors of those around them so perfectly that no one ever suspected a thing.

So maybe. But Symon didn't think so.

There was also that breed of people who really were better suited to be alone. There was a guy—Christopher Knight, also known as the "North Pond Hermit." He had lived for *twenty-seven years* alone in the woods of Maine. Much like Alex Kaine, Knight had survived by staying out of sight, stealing anything he needed from locals.

So, Alex Kayne could be that type. It was just that she'd

shown no signs of that, prior to the events at Populus, and the murder of her business partner.

Symon had another theory, but so far had no real evidence to support it.

He believed she was moving from city to city with a purpose. He believed she had something beyond escape and evasion motivating her—a reason for her existence.

He'd once read about a Japanese soldier in World War II. The Emperor had told the man to take to the jungles and fight, to evade capture, and to bring victory for Japan no matter what the cost or sacrifice. The solider, a loyal and honorable man, had taken an oath to do exactly as his Emperor had commanded. And for fifty years, even well after the end of the war, he and his men had hidden out, raiding villages and continuing the fight.

Even when the Emperor and his successors sent word, going so far as to drop flyers on the jungle, even sending emissaries to tell the man that the war was over, he fought on.

Eventually he was the only one of his men left, and still he continued his fight. Until, one day, a man who might best be described as a "hippie" went on a quest to find the soldier, to befriend him, and to perhaps convince him that the war really was over.

It had worked, eventually.

The soldier gave up the fight and returned to a world he barely recognized, where honor was no longer the driving force of Japanese culture.

When asked why he'd persisted, and had refused to believe even the Emperor when told the war was finished, the soldier had said that he'd been ordered by his Emperor to fight, no matter what. To fight until he could no longer fight. Honor propelled him.

That was the story, at least.

Eric had a different theory.

He believed the man had a *purpose*, and that purpose was what drove him.

He had his orders, and he fought. He committed everything to the war. And so, without the war, who was he? His purpose was to obey that order and to fight until the end. His *identity* was "the man who fights for his Emperor." So if he stopped that fight, he would no longer be himself. He would have to cast around and find a new purpose, a new identity.

Eric believed that Alex Kayne was engaged in the same sort of fight.

He'd seen her file, her profile, and everything ever written about her. She was accused of espionage, of betraying her country to the Russians, but nothing about her prior to those events at Populus had suggested anything like this was even remotely possible. She'd shown no signs of political zeal. No hint of sympathy to the Russians. Nothing about her made the espionage charges make sense, beyond the NSA tracing a Russian delegation to Populus on the day Adrian Ballard was killed.

What about the two Russians found murdered in a car nearby? Alex's fingerprints had been on the gun used to kill both men. Her bloody fingerprints had been recovered from the rear passenger door. Cut zip ties had been found on the floorboard.

Video from a local bodega showed her stealing a SIM card, but so far as Eric could tell that was just about the only crime they really had her on, from that day. The manager had even told them that he'd gotten a note and some cash to cover more than the cost of the SIM card, just a week or so later.

Symon just couldn't parse the idea that Alex Kayne was who the charges against her claimed her to be.

Still, she was wanted. She was a fugitive. And it was his job to bring her in.

As for why she was here, in Orlando, or why she was ever *anywhere* for that matter, Eric believed she was like that Japanese soldier.

She did what she did because she needed purpose for her life. She needed some sort of "why" for staying on the run. The only way to keep going, to keep eluding capture, to keep up this surely exhausting, nightmarish existence, was to have a reason. A damn good reason.

He wasn't sure what her literal actions were in each of the cities that Alex escaped to, but he believed that under it all was some purpose Alex had set for herself.

And if he could uncover that purpose, he believed, he could catch her.

CHAPTER EIGHT

ALEX BREATHED THROUGH IT.

That was the only thing she could do, really. Breathe, calm herself, regroup. This sort of thing had not been completely unexpected. She'd been waiting for it to happen. She'd been prepared.

Still, it had forced her to burn a perfectly good cover. And it forced her to readjust and relocate, which was a nuisance and a complication, especially now.

She couldn't use Airbnb again. Not while she was still in Orlando. The FBI had tracked her to the last one, and they'd be certain to check out every listing in the area, looking for new reservations.

Granted, Orlando—a high-traffic area for tourists, with people snagging such reservations daily, and by the thousands. It might take a while for them to sort out which reservation was hers. But her personal rule was, "once burned, move on." Scorched earth was the policy. So Airbnb was out.

Still, it wasn't her only resource.

She was currently parked at a Cracker Barrel restaurant, in

the back lot where a few RVs were taking advantage of the restaurant's free overnight parking. No one would think twice about someone parking and sleeping here for the evening. It was expected.

She parked the car under a spot of shade and then scraped the orange parking violation sticker from the driver's window. Then, looking around to make sure she wouldn't be noticed, she swapped out the plates and pulled away the thin coating of red vinyl that covered the car from bumper to bumper.

The Civic was now a dingy, mottled blue, thanks to the miracle of automotive wrapping.

She rolled the old plates into the wad of red vinyl and shoved the bundle under a stack of trash bags in the Cracker Barrel's dumpster. Even if anyone thought to look here, they'd be unlikely to even know what the wad of red plastic was, or what it signified.

That task done, Alex locked the car, grabbed her spare backpack from the trunk, and went inside. She would order some dinner, rest, and regroup.

It was nice to be greeted by friendly faces, and the waitress was pleasant and even a little concerned about Alex's well-being.

Alex realized she must look a little shaken. She *was* shaken. This had been a close call—really the first she'd had in quite a while, and so unexpected it rattled her.

She smiled at the waitress, said everything was fine, just a long drive in. Tourists made traffic crazy, right? She ordered an iced tea and a breakfast plate for dinner.

Comfort food, she told the waitress. And she'd meant it.

Alex had come in almost two hours before the restaurant closed, and once she was done with her meal, she lingered as long as was comfortable. She browsed the quaint little "country store" in the front of the restaurant, blending in with the throngs of patrons who were either killing time as they waited to be seated or doing some souvenir shopping.

It was a good place to get lost for a bit. No one noticed her with all the distractions around. And she could position herself so that she had an eye on the door, within reach of an exit.

Paranoia was the word of the day.

As closing time neared, however, and the crowd started to thin out, Alex knew it was time to get moving. She used the restroom before leaving and then retreated back to the Civic. She moved it closer to the RVs, as the sun set, and let the whir and white noise of their generators lull her to sleep.

It was a fitful night, which wasn't unexpected. She kept dreaming of FBI agents grabbing her and restraining her, pinning her down and preventing her from getting to any of her escape plans. She dreamt of zip ties and hand cuffs and Russians leering at her with blood pouring from wounds in their heads and necks. She dreamt that her hands were covered in blood, and no matter what she did, she could not wash it off. It clung to her, and to everything and everyone she touched.

She woke up in a panic, not knowing exactly where she was until the car's interior came into focus. The blue LED clock on the dash told her it was 4:26 AM.

Early. Nothing would be open until 8 AM at the earliest, and it would do no good to get moving prior to that.

But sleep was out of the question now. She'd always been an early riser anyway, and between nightmares and the discomfort of sleeping in a Civic, she knew it was done for.

She got out of the car, stretching, feeling her muscles protesting the previous night. She did some yoga poses, which quickly morphed into martial arts forms. Sort of an occupational hazard, at this point—since she'd been on the run, she'd been studying, practicing, and training like crazy in every form she could find online.

She'd even amped up practicing parkour—something she'd started as a way to keep fit, back before all of this had started. It had more or less been a lark, back then. But it had proven to be an invaluable skill. All the bruises, strained muscles, and sprained wrists and ankles had proven to be worth it, now that she was pretty good at moving fluidly through the tight spaces of the world.

After loosening up, she climbed back into the Civic, locking the door and turning on the engine. She'd slept with the engine off and the windows up, and even at night Orlando had supplied her with plenty of humidity and heat. The cool air flowing from the Civic's vents was welcome.

Still a few hours before life started moving around here. To pass the time, she picked up her phone from the center console —the spare phone she'd kept in the car, thank goodness—and brought up everything she had stored in the cloud regarding Abbey Cooper's case.

The strategic partner names she'd gotten from Uconic were all non-local, and mostly big corporations. Some were from different regions of the US, some were overseas. A number were government contacts and agencies, including foreign governments.

Where to start?

Always start with the strangest question, her grandfather had taught her.

One of the more puzzling things about this case was the theft of the arm itself.

Why would anyone do that? Abbey's arm was one of three, and perhaps the easiest one to obtain, but what was it about the arm that made it worth the trouble stealing? What could anyone do with it once they had it?

The technology was advanced, and it was proprietary, but it could be licensed by anyone who wanted it. Uconic had a sort of limited open-source license that allowed others to develop new technology using their platform. So corporate espionage seemed unlikely.

The government contracts would have given them full specs, prototypes, proprietary and specialized systems and components—there was zero need for any government to steal the arm.

What about independents?

Here, things got a bit more narrow. There were only three independent contractors on the list Alex had compiled. All three were in the Orlando area. When she looked deeper, they were primarily contractors aiding in Uconic's hardware and software development. One, however, was also licensing some of the arm's technology for uses outside of prosthetics.

She started digging deeper.

Shorelite Robotics, an Orlando-based technology firm, had made news over the past few years for work it was doing on behalf of NASA, and then later for contract work with SpaceX and other privately run space programs. They were heavily invested in developing robotics meant to assist astronauts on space walks, as well as automated robotics to help explore asteroids, comets, and even planetary surfaces.

Big deal stuff. And very exciting. But the company had run into a few hiccups along the way.

As independents, they struggled to keep up with firms that had better funding. Their advantage was their small size, and the ability to pivot and adapt quickly.

This was also their *disadvantage.*

Other firms were overcoming Shorelite's results by brute force, throwing money at the various challenges until new innovations emerged. It hadn't taken long for Shorelite to be overwhelmed by this strategy, and to start losing ground. Their partnership with Uconic was one of their last remaining lifelines.

So, that was a lead.

It still didn't explain why they would need to steal Abbey's arm, Alex knew. But it was the best lead she had for the moment. A direction. And right now, cramped and crammed into the driver's seat of a Honda Civic, having narrowly escaped the FBI, she'd take any decent direction she could get.

The sun rose, and Alex looked to see that it was after 6AM. She climbed out of the Civic again, stretched some more, stopped around to get the blood flowing, and then went back into the restaurant for coffee and breakfast.

It was going to be a long day, and among other things she had to pee.

She also had to hop online to find a new place to hunker down for the rest of her time in Orlando.

She might as well give the day a good start, with a belly full of scrambled eggs and bacon. And coffee, by God. There would be so much coffee.

BELLY FULL AND coffee coursing through her veins, Alex felt a little more like herself. Things were still skewed, the nerves were still a little jangled, but she was thinking clearly and was already at work on a plan.

First, she tackled the problem of a place to live.

Even if they assumed she was trying to get as far away as possible, the FBI would watch every Airbnb listing closely, in and around Orlando. So that was out.

Likewise, they'd monitor hotels and motels in the area. Or she would have done, if she were in their shoes. So it was a safe bet to assume they would.

Her overnight in Cracker Barrel's RV parking opened up some possibilities.

There were campgrounds in the area. RV parks, cabins, tent-camping—all of these were options. RV parks were on her resource list for their free WiFi and other amenities, including shower stalls and restrooms. And for the purely anonymous nature of the places. People came and went constantly, a continuous flow of transient, nomadic culture. No one was ever suspicious of a new face.

The trouble was that if the FBI thought to look there, they'd immediately ask about anyone who had checked in since yesterday. That would peg her quickly.

This timeline thing was the wall she kept bumping her head against.

Thinking about it, in the future she might start reserving a campsite in advance, as a backup. She could check in, park something in the space to hold it—maybe another getaway vehicle. A van would be good, solving both transportation and living in one swoop.

Good idea. Too late for it now, but it was an idea that had some merit. Next time.

For now, her options were starting to dwindle. Something she did not like. She spent a considerable amount of time making sure she had as many options open as possible, thinking ahead as far as she could, making a ridiculous level of arrangements for her escape. Now, somehow, she'd gotten caught in a gap, and she was kicking herself for not being fully prepared.

She considered couch surfing. There were a number of sites set up to connect travelers with people willing to share a space in their homes for a night or two. The situation was too impermanent for what Alex needed, though she'd used it a few times in the past, mostly for quick layovers.

Not ideal, but good in a pinch.

No, this time she was going to need space to spread out, as she worked this case. She needed to be able to spend long periods of time working from wherever she landed. She also needed a place to just relax, without worrying that someone might get suspicious and end up reporting her. She needed a safe haven.

Which meant she would have to resort to something extra sneaky, and even a little risky. Not to mention a teensy bit unethical.

But the more she thought about it, the more the idea made her smile.

She used QuIEK to make the arrangements. She even went to the trouble of back-dating the reservation, searching for a party that had canceled within the past few weeks. She spent time cloning their identities and adding details that would certainly skew any findings if someone happened to look. There were the ancillary arrangements to make as well, but they were necessary, just in case anyone looked.

It was a lot of time and work to set it up, and it wasn't without risk. A gamble. But heck, when in Rome...

Alex Kayne, you just evaded arrest by the FBI and committed a number of felonies! What's next?

"I'm going to Disney World," she said quietly, smiling and even laughing to herself.

She was officially booked at the Boardwalk Inn, along with her "husband" and their "two wonderful kids," and all part of a three week Disney vacation package that was just going to be one beautiful memory after another.

If the FBI thought to look for her there, she might just surrender. They would have earned it.

Still, on top of the room arrangements, Alex spent the next couple of hours setting up everything from a fake driver's license to prepaid credit cards to records of airfare between

Oklahoma and Orlando. Luckily, thanks to Disney being such a big presence in Orlando, she wouldn't have to bother setting up fake rental car records. Shuttles to and from the airport had no record of who was onboard, so they'd be a bit of camouflage. Nothing for the FBI to track.

With housing settled, it was time to make a few more arrangements.

Alex had moved the Honda Civic to a grocery store parking lot nearby and walked to the restaurant. It had served her well over the past couple of days, but even with new plates and a different paint job, it was too risky for her to keep using it.

Now she called an Uber, and when it arrived, she had it take her to the other side of town.

She'd get new wheels, eventually. First, she had a hair appointment to keep.

Silver hair was all the rage lately, and so the stylist never even blinked when Alex asked for her dark, shoulder-length hair to be cut short and tinted gray. Alex was still young by nearly every definition, but the silver hair did have the effect of aging her at first glance. If someone wasn't looking closely, they might assume she was a woman in maybe her late fifties.

Perfect.

She added large sunglasses to this, obstructing much of her face with a pair of designer lenses. For clothing she went with labels—a wardrobe plucked fresh from a summer fashion shoot. It was expensive. This run had delved deep into the balance on one of her prepaid cards, but she could more than afford it. Money was a number, after all, and she could work with numbers. She had plenty of reserve cash stashed around the city, and more than enough virtual cash on prepaid cards and stuffed into offshore accounts.

It was important to get this right.

She was adopting a new persona, which she'd done fairly

often over the past two years. The trick was to get the details right. There was a character involved. A story.

She called another Uber, and this time had it drop her off a few blocks from her real destination. She walked the rest of the way.

The lot was typical. Used vehicles sat in sun-baked rows, jammed so tight it was difficult to imagine being able to drive one out.

She had come in from the street, but now wound her way through the rows of cars until she came to the trailer being used as an office. She'd kept out of sight, so no one saw her approach. She wanted assumptions made, in case anyone ever asked about her.

"May I help you?" a salesman asked as she entered through the front door. He was alone, which did not necessarily mean there was no one else around.

"I need a car," she said, then took a roll of cash out of her bag. "And I'm in a hurry. I'm also not fond of paperwork."

He looked from the cash to her and then back again. He then glanced around, almost conspiratorially. "I can help," he said.

Alex smiled. She knew he could.

Twenty minutes later she was driving out of the parking lot on a "test drive," nearly ten grand lighter in the pockets, but it was worth it. The Lexus was older, but in good shape. A quick check of the engine had revealed nothing alarming. Everything was clean, hoses and belts looked good, the oil was practically invisible. The mileage was a little high, and the leather seats could have been in better condition, but Alex wasn't concerned much with trade in value. Reliable was the main consideration. Plus, the aesthetics fit with her new look. It was solid camouflage.

She pulled into the valet lane of a hotel just a couple of

miles from Disney—the sort of hotel that was a bit expensive for vacationing families, but still had bus service to the parks. Executives from out of town could take a day for some fun and overpriced souvenirs and still retreat to a place that wasn't overrun by screaming kids wearing mouse ears.

Alex took the valet ticket when offered and entered the hotel lobby. She wasted no time and went straight to the ground-floor restrooms. As quickly as possible she slipped into a stall, stood on the toilet, and hid the valet slip inside one of the drop ceiling panels. If she had to run, there'd be no risk of the valet slip being lost or left behind.

For good measure she shoved a roll of cash and a change of clothes into the space, as well as one of the pre-paid smartphones she'd purchased. She ensured this was turned off. The battery should stay charged for weeks, maybe even months.

One backup plan in place, and now she was down and walking back out just as someone entered the restroom. No strange looks or second glances were given. Just another day in Orlando.

In the lobby she got information from the concierge on the next bus to Disney Springs. She rode there, along with half a dozen other passengers, all absorbed in their smartphones, working even while on their way to the happiest place on Earth.

From Disney Springs she was able to catch a bus to the Boardwalk Inn, and rode along with quite a few tourists and families.

There was a moment—a pang of loneliness and regret—as she watched a young couple chatting with their daughter, who couldn't have been more than perhaps four years old. The little girl was appropriately attired in princess clothing, including a frilly pink ballet skirt and a fairy wand. She was very excited, bouncing up and down, asking when the bus would finally get to "Dizzy Wold."

Alex pried her eyes from the scene, looking instead at the passing scenery. She was glad she was wearing the oversized sunglasses.

Once she and the other passengers disembarked at the Boardwalk in, Alex checked in, then found her way to her room. She passed her keycard over the reader, then collapsed on the bed.

Tension ran out of her. She felt a tingle all over, like the aftermath being slapped. Her ears rang from the noise of the day. Her nerves, now having endured so much stress over the past 24 hours, felt jangly, as if they weren't sure where all the stimulus had gone.

It had been a long day. And a long night before that. And as evening approached over the Magic Kingdom and all the lands of its neighborhood, Alex let herself drift.

She had more arrangements to make. More backup plans to put into place. And, of course, she still had her client to think about. But for now, feeling safe and comfortable—for the moment, at least—she let herself relax. She'd get to the other details later. She'd get back to work later.

For now, she slept.

CHAPTER NINE

REFRESHED, refueled, and ready to get back to work, Alex sat in one of the plush chairs near a small bar in the hotel. She was surrounded by 1920s furnishings and decor, all well themed. She could almost fool herself into thinking she'd fallen back through time, to an era when technology and life itself were both simple and charming.

Easy to believe, when you didn't really live through it, she knew. Still, the nostalgia of this place was kind of a comfort.

There were families everywhere, with kids playing old board games, squealing with excitement, and parents chatting just as animatedly with friends or other family members. It was a warm and inviting environment—and it was depressing the *hell* out of Alex.

But it did make her feel safe enough to relax as she did her work.

She'd picked up a smart tablet from a pawnshop, using her new fake ID for their official records. She was using this to log into Smokescreen.

She checked the FBI database, intending to find out more about Agent Eric Symon.

He had quite a history.

After graduating from Quantico he'd gone on to work in various field offices, transferring frequently thanks to demand for his specialization.

Symon, it seemed, had a knack for tracking people. His fugitive recovery rate was the highest in agency history, and he'd maintained his streak for three years running.

He was an expert profiler, with multiple degrees in psychology, forensics, and criminal justice. He'd even authored a few books on the subject of profiling and the art of the manhunt, which Alex immediately purchased and downloaded.

Know your adversary.

Agent Symon was going to be a problem, she could tell. He was good at what he did, and he had a reputation for making unexpected and intuitive leaps when tracking someone. He was a strategic thinker, and resource thinker. Which meant he was good at planning and considering and looking at things from every angle, considering what the fugitive would have at his or her disposal, and how local resources might be used. In other words, he was good at thinking through all the angles, and considering all the routes of escape.

Just like Alex.

She'd have to stay alert.

She spent a few hours learning everything she could about Eric Symon and used QuIEK to dig a little further than public databases would allow. She got into his history, into what little presence he had online, into job and school records going all the way back to his early childhood. He was smart. No doubt about that. And he was *good*.

She kind of admired him.

His track record for finding fugitives actually extended well beyond his FBI career. In college, Symon had contributed valuable insight and data to local law enforcement that had helped track a number of bad guys on the run. He'd become known for it—the kid who could find fugitives. There were newspaper articles about him, and Alex felt sure that all of this had contributed to his career choice. It had certainly contributed to his choices for education, nudging him to major not only in criminology but in any related field he could.

Alex knew she'd have to keep a very close eye on him. If anyone had a shot at getting to her, it was Agent Eric Symon. Underestimating him would be a fatal mistake.

So... she would not underestimate him. She'd study him.

For now, though, she had a case of her own to solve. It was time to get back to work.

Shorelite Robotics had its offices in a rented building near Lake Mary, about an hour north of Orlando. She made arrangements for a rental car, using QuIEK to make it look like she had just flown in from out of state, and then used one of the Disney buses to get her to the airport.

It took longer than she would have liked, and she wasn't keen on showing her face at the airport, where there were sure to be agents on the lookout, and definitely cameras everywhere. She had the driver drop her close to the car rental return lanes, and then made her way up the steps of the parking garage, to the Gold Members pickup area.

From here she was able to pick the car she wanted, without having to deal with an agent. All arrangements had been made online, ahead of time.

She climbed behind the wheel of a Chevy Malibu, and when she got to the exit gate, she handed the attendant the ID and credit card she'd created.

It was a throwaway identity she would abandon as soon as she was done. The rental car would be recovered from a car wash in Lake Mary, paid for in full and with some extra care taken for vacuuming and deep interior detailing.

She'd make other arrangements to get home.

While she had the car, however, she put it to good use.

She drove to Lake Mary, keeping to the speed limit the whole way, and when she arrived, she took exit 101 toward Heathrow. A few turns and a couple of miles later, she pulled into the parking lot of Shorelite Robotics and left the rental sitting in a shaded spot.

She'd read up on this place, and she'd been impressed. It was remarkable how much they'd accomplished since their founding, just ten years earlier. One of the founders had strong connections with NASA, having worked for the space agency for nearly three decades, and this had surely helped grease the wheels for government contracts and other options.

When Elon Musk and his team started looking for partners for SpaceX, Shorelite had managed to get on a short list. Their NASA connection and other resources had given them an in, and they'd pushed it as far as they could. It had paid off, getting them a contract and establishing them as a partner. A lucrative start.

Alex entered through the automatic glass doors in front, and was greeted by a well-dressed man in his late twenties, wearing a vest and bow tie, his hair slicked and well-coiffed.

"Welcome to Shorelite!" he said enthusiastically, leaning forward and smiling at her. "How may I help you?"

Alex returned his smile. "My name is Bonnie Miller," she said, producing an ID badge. "I'm supposed to meet with Tim Davis in..." she made a show of taking out her phone to look at the time before placing it on the counter near a thumbprint scanner. "Oh, in about ten minutes!" she said, flustered. "I had hoped I'd have time to... um... visit the ladies room."

The young man laughed lightly. "That's no problem, Ms. Miller. Just put your thumb on the scanner, and we'll clear you to enter. The restrooms are just down the hall, to your left."

Alex smiled gratefully, then placed her thumb on the scanner. There was a brief pause, and then she heard a beep.

"All good!" the receptionist said. "Mr. Davis is on the second floor. Just ask for him at the upstairs reception desk, when you're ready."

Alex smiled, then took her phone and followed the directions to the restrooms. She slipped inside and locked the door behind her. She hurriedly pulled the white lab coat out of her bag and then stashed her own clothes inside. She unclipped the shoulder straps of the bag and stuffed them inside as well, zipping the bag closed and grasping the smaller handles, carrying the bag like a briefcase. She slipped a Shorelite visitor badge out of her pocket and clipped it to the lab coat, then pulled on a pair of glasses with clear lenses—an unnecessary affect, but they helped her get into character.

This was different from her run at the Uconic offices. For a start, she had no idea what she was looking for here. She'd accessed everything she could find, both within Shorelite's own databases and on the web. She'd peeked into files and profiles of the firm in the networks of other businesses. And while she'd found a great deal of information about both the UUP8 and UUPX prosthetics, she hadn't really found anything that would work as a motive for Shorelite to steal one of the prototypes.

She was grasping.

She moved through the ground floor hallway and used the elevator to go to the second floor. The building only had the two floors, with the second floor largely being offices and a library. The library housed documentation and reference material used by the company's research team and included a secure room where classified and sensitive documents were stored.

Moving through Shorelite was a bit more challenging than her incursion into Uconic, despite the security being considerably lighter.

The problem was, Shorelite was small, with less than a hundred employees. The chances were high that someone would spot her and ask who she was. She'd concocted a cover story, but whether it held up well was still something of a crapshoot.

She was starting to wonder about this plan.

Was she overcompensating? After her run-in with Agent Symon, she'd felt a bit off. Rattled. Despite having made her escape, and all of her preparations working just as she'd planned, she couldn't help feeling as if she'd blown it. She'd had close calls with the FBI, police, even the NSA over the past two years, but this one had felt... different.

Agent Symon was different.

He'd not only gotten shockingly close to her—literally laying hands on her—he'd done it in a way that was similar to what Alex would have done herself. He had watched her, had figured out her patterns, and had prepared. She'd just prepared a little better.

This time.

Would she be able to count on that next time?

If that experience had rattled her, she might be making mistakes. This move, infiltrating Shorelite with no real purpose for being here, was almost certainly one of those mistakes.

She had nearly convinced herself to abandon the whole operation and get back to her hotel, to regroup and start again, when she turned a corner of the stacks and literally bumped into Tim Davis, Shorelite's founder and CEO.

"I'm very sorry," he smiled at her. "I..." He paused, a curious expression on his face. "I don't recognize you," he said.

Alex smiled and shook her head, then stuck out her hand. "We haven't met yet, sorry. I'm Bonnie Miller. I got in this morning, and only just arrived. I'm very sorry for being late, Mr. Davis. I wasn't expecting the traffic on I-4. I guess I under-estimated the appeal of Disney World."

Davis took her hand, gripping it lightly and looking at her with unmasked suspicion. "We had an appointment?"

She blinked, making a show of being a bit flustered. "I... hope so..." she took out her phone and opened the calendar app. "I have it on my calendar," she mumbled, then closed her eyes and took a deep breath, letting it out with a sigh. "Next week," she said, raising a hand to push up her glasses and rub her eyes. "I am so sorry, Mr. Davis. I must have mixed up the dates! It looks like I'm here a week early!"

Davis had taken out his own phone, and was checking his calendar, where he would absolutely find an appointment to meet with a Ms. Bonnie Miller, one week from the day. He looked up at her and shook his head. "That's quite a mixup," he said.

"I've been in four countries on three continents in the past three months," she said, yawning. "I apologize. I'm lucky to know what year it is. Still 2008, right?" She smiled again, and to her relief Davis smiled as well.

"Fortunately, no," he said. "Well, I'm sorry there was a mixup, Ms. Miller, but I'm afraid I can't let you have access to the library just yet. You'll have to return next week. To be honest, I'm not even sure what our meeting was about. I've completely blanked on this appointment."

"I'm a consultant," Alex said. "Sort of a liaison, here on behalf of Uconic. I'll be in their offices for most of the month. That's probably where I'll go from here. So embarrassing!"

"Oh, don't be embarrassed!" Davis said. "I know what it's like to get traveler's brain fog."

She smiled, nodding. "Now I just have to work out where I'm going to work for the day. I have a lot of email and other work I need to get to. This has really cost me some time!"

Davis frowned, considering. "You're with Uconic? I was going to arrange a meeting with some of their people, anyway. Must have been in the back of my mind. Well, since you're here, I'm happy to set you up with a temporary workspace, if you need it. No sense fighting I-4 traffic all the way back to Orlando."

"That would be amazing," Alex said with relief.

Davis smiled and led her away, through the library to one of the small temporary offices. It was a basic workspace, with a desk and chair, a lamp on the desk, and some artwork on the walls. A comfortable space, with a door and a large window overlooking the library, and adjustable blinds for privacy. No window to the outside, but there was a lush, green plant on a stand in one corner.

"It isn't much," Davis said. "But you're welcome to work from here for the day. If you need anything, hit zero on the phone to ring reception."

"I really appreciate this," she said as they shook hands again. "I promise, I'm not usually so scattered."

He waved a hand. "It happens. Have a good day, Ms. Miller."

He left, closing the door behind him. She watched as he made his way out of the library and down a corridor, turning and disappearing.

She opened the door and then closed the blinds before pulling the door closed again.

She wasn't entirely sure that Davis had completely fallen

for her story. He seemed a little hesitant and wary. But she'd bought herself some time, at least.

There were several other employees in the library, spreading documents over tables or browsing the stacks. Many had laptops, and were paired off to discuss a variety of topics.

There was enough activity in the space that it acted as camouflage while Alex exited the little office and moved toward the secured room.

Here, she stopped short.

She had opened a lot of secured doors over the past two years. Almost all of them had some form of scanner or electronic security she could manipulate. QuIEK was essentially a digital skeleton key.

For the first time, however, she was faced with a dilemma for which she had not fully prepared.

The door had an old fashioned keyed deadbolt.

No sensors. No keypads. No retina scans. Nothing she could manipulate with QuIEK. What kind of technology firm was this?

Possibly a brilliant one, if the goal was to keep someone like her from mucking about in the works.

She passed by the door as if it had not been her destination. She knew from the floorplans that there was a kitchenette at the end of this hall, where employees could make coffee or keep food in a fridge.

Office kitchens were on her resource list.

Employees of companies such as this could always be counted on to bring a variety of tools, gadgets, and utensils from home. There were usually emergency kits and medicine kits, restocked regularly with pain relievers and other medicines.

The setup was fairly basic for the break room. There was a refrigerator on one wall and a sink mounted in a counter that had two sets of drawers and cabinet doors. Above that was a hanging cabinet that served as a cupboard, filled will a variety of reusable coffee mugs.

Against the opposite wall was a photocopier, and a small cabinet filled with office supplies. A cork board was mounted on the wall above this, and had dozens of papers tacked to it, alerting employees to medical benefits, rules about copier use, and company activity calendars.

Alex opened one of the cabinet doors and found stacks of small boxes filled with paper clips. She opened one of these and spilled some clips into her palm.

Another box contained a number of ballpoint pens. She took a pen out and examined it, clicking it a couple of times. She pulled at the metal clip of the pen, bending it until she could work it free from the pen's housing. She put the pen, the clip and some paperclips into the pocket of her lab coat. She then took one of the paperclips and straightened it and used a pair of scissors to bend the tip into a slight angle.

She went back to the locked room and looked to see if anyone was nearby.

With the coast clear, for the moment, she slid the bent paperclip into the keyhole, and used the clip from the pen as a tension wrench. She started raking the bent tip of the paperclip over the tumblers inside the lock, keeping tension on the cylinder using the pen clip. She did this in a hurry, not quite feeling whether the pins inside were meeting the sheer point, but not having time to feel her way through this, anyway.

She was a bit rusty at this—a skill she hadn't had to use much over the past couple of years. But in a moment she had the pins aligned and could turn the cylinder freely.

There was a click, and she was able to open the door.

The beeping started immediately, but she'd been ready for this. She took out her phone, held it close to the alarm panel on the wall, and ran a protocol via QuIEK.

Finally, some modern security.

The beeping stopped, and Alex closed and locked the door behind her.

She was in.

The trouble was, she still had no idea what she was looking for.

She started opening file drawers and cabinets, quickly scanning everything she encountered. She used her phone to grab video of everything as she went. It was much faster to shoot 4K video that she could pull stills from later, rather than shooting individual photos. The video was automatically backed up to the cloud, where she could parse through it at will using the bigger screen of her laptop or tablet.

The trouble was, while she was uncovering quite a bit of data, she wasn't finding anything worth all the risk and effort of getting in here.

Shorelite had legitimate access to any documentation or data regarding UUP8 and UUPX. They had prototypes of their own—though not entirely complete—and they had contracts to use the technology in a variety of ways. They had no discernible motive for stealing the arm, as far as Alex could determine.

This was turning out to be a bust.

Maybe she really had let Agent Symon rattle her. Maybe the close call really had thrown her off her game.

She sighed and made her decision. It was time to leave. She'd have to find a new trail to follow. This whole thing had been a risk for no good reason. She would get out of here, and take some time to "reset," to shake off the near-miss and start thinking smart again.

She tucked her phone into her pocket and then cracked the door open to peek out and check if the coast was clear.

The coast was not clear.

"Ma'am," a security guard said, putting a hand out to push the door open. "Come with me, please."

Behind the guard was Tim Davis.

For the second time in two days, Alex had slipped up and let herself be cornered.

This time, she didn't have a rope to swing away on.

CHAPTER TEN

THE ORLANDO FIELD office of the FBI was located in Maitland, in a building that housed several additional government agency offices, including the IRS.

Agent Eric Symon wasn't fond of the place. Or of sitting in offices in general, for that matter. It was a necessary evil that came with the badge. Eventually, you owed butt-in-chair time.

He had debriefed, answered questions, and given speculation on what he thought might be Alex Kayne's motives and her plans. He knew these were just guesses at best and bullshit at worst. For two years the FBI had been on the trail of Alex Kayne, and by now she was more of a source of embarrassment than anyone that the FBI considered a serious threat.

Of course, embarrassing the FBI was enough. And the allegations against her *were* serious. And both were reason enough to have the Bureau's top resources on the case.

At the risk of being immodest, Symon knew that he was one of these top resources. Which was why it was confounding to think he hadn't been a part of the manhunt from the start.

"Why wasn't I brought in sooner?" Symon had asked back at Langley.

He'd regretted it almost the instant the words left his mouth, but he stood by it. And his superiors had wasted no time in reminding him that he was not the only agent with a good track record and a skill for bringing in fugitives. They advised him to keep his ego in check, and to focus on doing his job.

He had nodded, without reply. But he'd already figured out why he was here now, in Orlando, finally brought into the hunt for Alex Kayne after two years in the wind.

It was Crispen.

Former FBI Director Matthew Crispen was currently serving a prison term for treason, as a result of his role in a terrorist plot. It had been a messy affair all around, and a tremendous black eye for the FBI. And everyone who had worked closely with Crispen had been under suspicion ever since.

That included Agent Eric Symon.

He'd been absolved of any wrongdoing, or even having any knowledge of Crispen's activities. But the FBI could have a long and suspicious memory.

A black mark on the agency's reputation was something it took seriously. Even in the wake of political fallout, thanks to bizarre and unpredictable behavior in the White House, the FBI maintained a tight grip on its reputation and integrity. Crispen's betrayal had created waves of repercussion that still rippled through the agency all these years later.

Symon had decided that the best way to fight back against unfair scrutiny and unwarranted distrust was to be the best damn agent out there. Excellence came from focus, he knew, and so he'd focused on something he'd already shown some promise for—he'd decided he would be the best fugitive hunter in the agency.

Symon continued to hone the discipline and skills he'd learned from his careers in local law enforcement and the FBI. He studied like mad, pouring over old cases, reading reports on successful track-and-capture operations. In his off hours, he interviewed both agents and fugitives alike. He studied psychology, auditing every class he could.

He turned his focus fully toward finding fugitives and bringing them to justice.

He'd gotten very good at it.

Which was why, two years after Alex Kayne had made a run for it, he'd been slightly baffled that he was only now being called to help in the search. He tried not to let it be an ego thing... but it was kind of an ego thing.

But here he was. Finally. They'd called him from the bench and given him the bat.

And he'd whiffed it.

Scrutiny on this case, and his involvement in it, was going to be heavy. He was going to get lectured, when things went wrong. He knew this. But he'd managed to build some buffer into the whole thing—he'd pitched that Alex Kayne was a special case, and that it might take more than the usual approach.

There was a lot to back this up. Kayne was a genius, after all. Not just because of her technical background—which was significant. She also showed a clear proclivity for learning new skills, thinking strategically ten to twenty moves ahead, and seeing the whole playing field in a sort of 4D perspective.

Symon was good. But so was Kayne.

This might take more than a couple of shots.

They'd bought his pitch. Or seemed to, at least. And now,

here he was. A whiff of the bat on the first swing, but still a couple of strikes to go.

After enduring some cold and pointed remarks from the local honcho, Symon had been duly warned and chastised, and then turned loose. The directive still stood. Find Alex Kayne. Bring her to justice. No more screwups.

Symon had *yessirred* his way out of the Director's office and now stood on the edge of a small, perfectly round man-made pond behind the government building, contemplating his next move.

Beyond the pond was I-4, teeming with traffic as always. The noise of cars rushing by in both directions washed over him, a white wall that blocked out nearly everything else and let his mind just mellow and drift. Ducks bobbed on the surface of the pond, oblivious to the trappings of humanity around them.

A sign next to the water warned of snakes and alligators. Symon glanced at the grass under his feet and traced the line of the water, looking for anything that might be dangerous. A dark, slithering shape moved deeper into he tall reeds just fifteen feet from him, and he shivered a little despite the humid heat of the Orlando day, then took a couple of steps back.

"Agent Symon," a woman's voice said from behind him.

He turned to see Agent Mayher walking toward him. She had a file in her hand and gave it to him as the two of them took a seat at a picnic table in the shade.

Mayher took off her coat. "Any reason we're out here instead of in the air conditioning?"

Symon chuckled. "I'm not a fan of cubicles." He looked over the file, which was thick with reports and surveillance photos. He'd seen much of this before. It held nothing new for him. He looked up at Mayher. "It's the same story, over and over."

"She's good," Mayher nodded.

Symon's eyebrows went up. "You sound like you admire her."

Mayher, a little flustered, started, "No... that's not..."

He laughed. "Don't feel bad about it. I admire her, too."

Mayher blinked. "She's a criminal."

"A fugitive," Symon corrected. "She hasn't been convicted of anything yet. And to be honest, the evidence seems a little sketchy."

"Her partner was colluding with the Russians, we have evidence for that. Her company was supplying them with classified technology, and she ran the second she was accused of Adrian Ballard's murder, and of espionage. She stole classified tech and ran."

"Classified tech that she invented," Symon said. "And that she's made clear she did not want falling into Russian hands."

"Or American hands," Mayher added.

Symon nodded. "That does seem to be the case." He thought for a moment, then sifted through the file in front of him. He pulled out what he was looking for and spread the papers in front of Mayher.

"This is the contract between Populus and the US government," Mayher said, peering at the papers. "What am I looking for?"

"Look at the signature," Symon said, tapping the spot with his finger.

"Adrian Ballard," Mayher replied.

"All of them," Symon nodded. "Every page, every contract, every memo. All of it came from Ballard, counter signed by members of their advisory board. Not a single signature from Alex Kayne."

"So you're saying she didn't know about the contracts?"

"And she likely wouldn't have agreed to sign them," Symon

said. He sifted through file again, and when he didn't find what he was looking for he took out his phone and swiped a few times, then turned the phone for Mayher to see.

"Have you read this? It's a paper Kayne wrote, just a year prior to going on the run. She outlined all the ways in which quantum data encryption could help everyday people. She wanted the technology to be openly available for everyone to use, not just governments. She expressly spoke out against government control of technology like this, saying that the only way to preserve liberty was to empower individuals."

Mayher looked up from the phone, a critical expression on her face. "You really do admire her. You sound like a fan."

"I like civil liberty," Symon said, then leaned in slightly. "I swore an oath to protect it."

"Doesn't matter," Mayher said. "She's a fugitive."

"And my job... our job... is to bring her in," Symon agreed. "And to do that, we need to understand her. The *real* her, not just the picture we've been handed."

Mayher thought about this and shook her head. "Ok, yeah. You're right. I hadn't thought of it that way. We have her file, we have reports from other agents, but if it's all built on a bad assumption, it hampers our search."

"Exactly," Symon said. "So our job now is to figure out her 'why.' Why is she here in Orlando? Why hasn't she run, now that she knows we're on to her? Why does she keep repeating this particular pattern?"

"Pattern?" Mayher asked.

He looked at her, then closed the folder and rested his phone on top of it.

"Forget her file for a minute. It's mostly speculation, anyway. The facts weirder." He looked out at the water and the busy interstate, then back to Mayher.

"Two years ago Alex Kayne gets accused of murder and

espionage. Her immediate response is to kill two Russian agents and go on the run. But then, just three months later, she surfaces, still in San Francisco, where the risk of getting caught would be highest. She cons her way into a secure facility and steals information and materials that later turn up as evidence against that company's CEO. A month later there's evidence of her being in Wyoming, where she caused a dust up with local authorities but was more or less forgotten when they suddenly discovered a human trafficking ring in their midsts. Two months after that she's in Manhattan, where a real estate scam gets exposed and thousands of people get their money back from a guy who'd been selling fake development properties."

Mayher listened, leaning forward with her arms on the picnic table, her hands knitted together. "So... what? You're saying she's a modern day Robin Hood? Righting wrongs for the little guy?"

"More like a one-woman A-Team, but yeah, I think that's the gist of it."

Mayher shook her head, then looked at him with a hard expression. "How? I can see there's some kind of link, but to do the sort of things you're talking about she'd either have to be a superhero or she'd have to have a team supporting her. We've never found any evidence that she's working with anyone else. And she's got some pretty good moves," Mayher self-consciously moved a hand to her shoulder, her fingers gliding over the spot where one of the tank top straps had gotten twisted. "But she's not exactly Spider-man."

Symon shrugged. "You're the one who told me about her swinging escape."

Mayher shook her head. "The point is, it doesn't matter. She can't make up for her crimes with good deeds. She's still a wanted fugitive, and it's still our job to bring her in."

Symon nodded. "Absolutely. It is. And we will. She's had a

good run of it for two years. But now we're on the case, and I haven't failed to bring anyone in yet. I don't plan to start. But what we're talking about is her *motive*. We need to know how she sees herself if we're going to predict what she does next."

Mayher blinked. "You're right." She shook her head. "I keep doing that. Overlooking that and getting caught up in thinking about her like any other fugitive. Why do I do that?"

"Because we're used to pursing bad guys who are *actually* bad guys," Symon shrugged. "The thought that someone would risk their freedom, while on the run from the FBI, just to help someone else... that throws us for a loop. We have to rethink the paradigm, and that causes cognitive dissonance." He saw from her expression that she wasn't quick clicking with what he'd said. "Changing how you think about a problem hurts, and sucks, and it's very uncomfortable."

She nodded, but said nothing.

He stood up. "You hungry? I could go for a burger."

She also stood up, and took the file, handing Symon his phone just as it started to vibrate.

He took it and checked the message on the screen. "Burger will have to wait," he said. "She's been spotted. Not far from here." He looked at her. "You're with me."

She nodded and then followed him to a black sedan in the parking lot.

They sped away, moving onto the highway and toward Lake Mary.

Mayher called in, coordinating with other agents and the police.

Symon was silent for most of the drive, and as Mayher hung up she said, "If she sees herself as the hero, then that means there's someone here in Orlando that needs her help."

Symon nodded.

"Those other cases... there were victims. Real victims."

"Yes," Symon said. "Real victims. Real innocent people who needed help and got it."

"So if we stop Kayne, we might be keeping her from helping someone else."

Symon said nothing, but this was exactly what had been on his mind, as he'd watched ducks swim in a pond that might have snakes and alligators hiding under its surface, waiting to attack.

Who ends up getting away with something, when we take down Alex Kayne?

The question hung over him as they rode in silence for the rest of the drive.

CHAPTER ELEVEN

"Who are you?" Davis asked her.

They were seated in the security office. The guard had left her and Davis alone, upon the request of the CEO but against his better judgement.

The police were on their way, and Davis wanted a moment to see if he could find out which of his competitors was after Shorelite's proprietary data.

Alex said nothing to dissuade this idea. It was much better if everyone was working from assumptions, and corporate espionage might have enough merit to derail the FBI for a bit.

"Nobody," Alex said. "Just passing through."

He shook his head. "Bonnie Miller? Come on. If you're going to use a fake name, you can come up with something better than a slanted reference to a 70s sitcom.

Alex actually smiled at that. "You'd be surprised how often that works."

"What were you after?" he asked her. "You can tell me that, at least. You mentioned Uconic when you got here. Are you trying to steal something from their UUP program? UUPX?"

Alex studied him for a moment and made a decision.

It was risky. It might give the FBI a lead she didn't want them to have. But this little operation had been a bust and here was a chance to salvage it. And, hopefully, to find a way to make this right for her client.

"No, not steal it. In fact... what do you know about Abbey Cooper?"

There was a blink, a brief instant in which Davis revealed he knew quite a bit about Abbey Cooper. He looked Alex over, then shook his head. "So what are you, another private investigator?"

"Something like that," she said.

"We told the last one, we know nothing about who took her arm. We don't know why anyone would want to, honestly. It's as bizarre to us as it is to the authorities."

"Not so bizarre to Abbey," Alex said. "Someone needed that arm for something. You're saying the PI she hired came here too?"

"No one told you?" Davis asked.

"I haven't talked to anyone who was looking into the case. But I've read the files. There's no mention of Shorelite in anything official."

Davis glanced at the door. "No," he said quietly. "There wouldn't be. Listen, whoever you are, you're in big trouble. I'm sorry for Ms. Cooper's predicament. But Shorelite had nothing to do with the theft. We'd have no reason to take her arm. None. We could actually build a replacement for her, if it didn't violate our contract with Uconic."

Alex blinked. "You could, couldn't you..." She thought about this. There had been something nagging at her, clinging to her brain like a spider trying to stay hidden. Now, hearing Davis, something shifted in the mental catalog she was running, the landscape of details for this case.

"How long before the police get here?" she asked.

Davis shook his head. "Not long. I was hoping you'd be willing to tell me something. I was hoping to get something on a competitor, nail them for corporate espionage. Now that I know you were hired by Abbey Cooper, I'm not even sure how I feel about it."

"You could always tell the police it was a big mistake, and let me go," Alex smiled.

Davis shook his head and chuckled. "No, I don't think I can do that. I'm not at all certain I can trust you. I watched how you got into that room." He glanced over at the table where her phone sat, locked. "You have something on that phone. But honestly, I was more impressed by how you picked the lock. Very old-world spy of you."

"I've picked up some skills here and there."

"I noticed."

She sighed. "Listen, you're right. You have no real reason to trust me. But I want to ask you for a favor, anyway."

Davis looked amused. "A favor. Ok, what is it? No guarantees."

"No guarantees," she nodded. "But for Abbey Cooper's sake, I'm going to ask you to tell the police and anyone else who shows up that this *was* corporate espionage. Don't let them know that I was here looking into the theft."

Davis studied her, looking a little perplexed. He shook his head. "Why not? Wouldn't that actually help you? I mean, you'll be arrested, but if they knew you were working for Abbey..."

"They can't know I'm working for Abbey," Alex said. "If they did, it would put her in danger."

This, strictly speaking, wasn't entirely true. The person it would put in danger was Alex herself. But it would effectively derail the whole case and maybe make it impossible for Alex to continue helping her. Best-case scenario, she would have to make a run for it and come back later, when things calmed down, to finish the case. But the risk of getting caught would go up exponentially at that point. Any contact she had with Abbey, anything she did that could be linked to Abbey, would make her vulnerable.

To help Abbey, this needed to be a secret.

Davis was watching her, and she could see he'd made a decision. He nodded. "Ok. Corporate espionage. Or, at least, I won't mention Abbey Cooper. We have nothing that would link her to this, anyway. So I'll just keep this part of our conversation off the record."

Alex nodded. "Thank you."

"But you realize it doesn't change anything, right?" Davis asked. "The police are still not their way. You'll still be arrested. I have to file charges."

"I know," she said. "That's what makes this a little easier, even though I don't really want to do it."

Davis blinked. "Do... what exactly?"

She looked around the room. She was handcuffed to the chair she was in. Davis was close, about two feet in front of her. The room had no windows and only one door. The security guard was outside.

Her options were limited.

She screamed.

"What... what are you...?" Davis started.

The security guard burst into the room, his hand on his holstered weapon.

Alex rolled, bringing the chair up and spinning it toward the guard, catching him in the brow with one of the metal legs. He fell back, and Alex leaped forward, pressing the chair down on his chest.

She slid the cuff down the chair's arm, to where it met the

base of the seat, and then yanked hard. The metal brace snapped away from the plastic seat, and she pulled the cuff free.

Davis, who had been startled into standing and had stepped back during the melee, suddenly rushed forward, trying to grab and hold her.

It was just instinct on his part. Alex didn't want to hurt him. And so she sidestepped, bring her knee up into his stomach and knocking the wind from him.

She grabbed her phone from the table and slid it into her back pocket. Then she grabbed the lab coat that she'd been wearing, from where it was draped over another chair. She pulled this on as she hurried from the room.

She had only minutes, she was sure.

The security office, where she'd been held, was on the first floor, and so it was easy to breeze out into the lobby, past the dapper receptionist, and through the glass doors leading to the parking lot outside.

The rental car was still in its spot in the shade, but she left it sitting there. They would have all manner of alerts on that car, she knew. She wouldn't make it three blocks before they'd have her.

On the street, she saw a police cruiser pulling into the parking lot.

Worse, she saw a black sedan parking on the street.

Options were again becoming narrow.

The officers pulled to the front of the building, lights flashing. She rushed to them.

"She's broken free!" Alex shouted to them. "She has Mr. Davis as a hostage! In the security office!"

The officers rushed out of the cruiser, weapons drawn, and ran into the building.

Alex followed them.

As they rushed inside and asked the receptionist for details, Alex moved quickly through a side door, passing her phone over the scanner plate to unlock it. The door led into the cavernous expanse that housed labs and workshops.

She let the door close and heard the lock click. Anyone coming in would need to use a security badge, which would help slow them down, if only for a few seconds.

She'd need those few seconds.

Here, among rows of machinery and equipment, people were working diligently on assembling a variety of robotic devices. There were people soldering, using pneumatic tools, bolting together bits of metal and plastic and polymers, and performing other tasks she couldn't even guess at.

Alex raced through the workshop floor until she came to the large, rolling doors at the far end. This was where deliveries would be made, as well as how engineers would get large equipment in and out of the workshop.

She hit the button to engage this door, and it began to open in a slow, noisy rise. Workers looked up, wondering about the sudden change in routine. Something interesting was happening, but no one made any move to stop her.

She rolled under the door when the gap was wide enough, then sprinted into the bushes behind the facility.

There was a fence here, separating Shorelite and neighboring businesses from a hotel parking lot next door. She quickly scaled the fence and was just about to make it over the top when a woman shouted from below.

"Alex Kayne! This is the FBI! Climb down and lay on the ground with your hands on your head!"

She looked back and saw a female agent with her weapon trained on Alex.

She recognized her. Tank top.

She'd been with Agent Symon at the park.

Without a word Alex rolled, letting gravity take her to the ground on the other side. She landed with a thud that knocked the wind from her, and she heard a shot from the other side of the fence. The bushes and brush helped hide her for the moment, preventing the agent from getting a clean shot.

Alex recovered, getting to her feet and running full tilt for the hotel. Along the way she shed the lab coat and clipped the other side of the cuffs to her wrist. She'd have to work out a way to remove them later, but for the moment she hoped that any onlookers would just assume they were a fashion choice.

She made it to the hotel's parking lot and ducked among the cars. It wouldn't be long before the FBI got here, fence or no fence. She'd be surrounded quickly. She had nowhere else to run.

Everything you need is right in front of you.

The voice of her grandfather. In times when things started to look bleak and hopeless, he almost always drifted in, like an Obi Wan in overalls spooning out practical wisdom and making her take a beat to think.

He was right.

Two cars over, she spotted exactly what she needed.

It was going to be just a little tricky, but she could do it.

She moved and took her phone out of her pocket. She crouched, and got to work, running QuIEK while she focused on breathing, calming, staying level.

She heard a thunk from the car door and opened it.

She hadn't been in a Tesla in over two years, but it felt as familiar as home.

She used QuIEK to bypass the security system, and to start the engine. In moments she was pulling out onto the street and putting as much distance between her and the FBI as she could manage at a reasonable an unhurried pace.

She was counting on the fact that the FBI and the police

were focused on the Shorelite facility, with no eyes on this parking lot. They would surely check security footage and spot the car she'd taken, but by then, she hoped, she should be miles away.

Her nerves, her stomach, everything was screaming. Anxiety was building to a point where she thought her head might pop. But she kept things steady.

When she'd managed to get a few miles from the hotel she started working her way onto the highway. And when she reached I-4 she drove until she got to a rest stop, then parked the Tesla between two large trucks. She had already arranged an Uber to pick her up, and over the next three hours she cycled through a variety of drivers take her in hops to coffee shops and restaurants and shopping centers all along I-4.

She was playing a shell game. Keep moving. Keep in motion. Fake, feint, and feign. A couple of times she called for an Uber and gave the driver fifty bucks to just drive to any random location and end the fare.

Eventually, after one last Uber and then a long walk to a hotel, she boarded a bus back to Disney Springs, and from there got another ride back to the Boardwalk Inn.

She'd made enough changeovers and swaps and doublebacks that she felt it would be fairly impossible for anyone to have tracked her this far. But given her track record over the past few days, she couldn't be entirely sure she hadn't made some mistake.

If so... so be it. All of this had been exhausting. The stress, the anxiety, the paranoia had all taken its toll.

Back at the resort, she slipped into the room and collapsed on her bed. A moment later she sat up and used an under wire from her bra to work into the handcuffs and unlock them. She stowed them in her bag. They might come in handy at some point. Or otherwise she'd toss them somewhere later.

She peeled her clothes off and slipped into a long, hot shower. Then, toweling herself dry, she collapsed on the bed again and was asleep in seconds.

She woke up with the room dark, and the sounds of Board-walk night life coming in muffled waves into her room. In its way, it was comforting. But also a little bizarre.

So much joy and freedom. Everyone on the boardwalk was going about their lives as if Alex hadn't almost been arrested and thrown into a deep, dark hole somewhere. The incongruity of the whole thing was like falling into an icy pool. She was awake now, tired or not.

Today had been a disaster.

The second disaster in three days, and she'd nearly gotten caught by both.

Worse, she'd made no real progress on the case whatsoever, and she was in real jeopardy of letting Abbey down.

This wasn't working. She was being *reactive* instead of *proactive*. That was when mistakes started to pile up.

She had to change her approach.

She dressed and left the room in search of some place to get a meal and to recharge. She couldn't face the loneliness of her room at the moment. The existential crisis of being isolated right now was enough to overcome the growing paranoia about being in public.

Tonight she'd eat, drink, and try to be merry.

Tomorrow, she'd come up with a new plan.

It was time to get back to playing smarter.

CHAPTER TWELVE

THE WORST PART was that she had to change her hair color *again*.

That agent, the woman who had shot at her, had seen her. She wasn't likely to miss a detail like a new haircut and hair color. So this look was burned.

That was a bummer, because Alex rather liked it. She didn't often have a chance to look fashionable or distinguished, while still remaining low profile. Usually she had to blend in, be bland and undistinguished. It had been this way for two years.

She'd had high hopes for keeping this look for a while.

But one of the advantages of it was that she could easily have the color changed.

She found a stylist conveniently located on the resort property. Their rates were alarmingly high, but the convenience of not having to go out in public—where the risk of being spotted went up—made them the perfect choice.

She had the stylist aim for something dark and rich, with hints of her original color so she wouldn't have to return for touch-ups. She also added extensions, giving her hair more length and body.

The result was that she looked like an entirely different person at a glance. The FBI was trained to recognize facial features, even beyond things like glasses and hairstyles, so she wouldn't necessarily pass close scrutiny. But the obvious markers were obliterated. It would be tougher to pick her out on video surveillance, or at a distance.

This job was turning out to be a lot more physically active than most others, so it was time to consider her wardrobe. She frequently had to change her look to blend in with various environments, but from this point forward she'd make sure she had something under her clothes that would let her not only quick-change, but would flow with her for quick movements.

She visited a high-end fitness store that was a quick Uber ride from Disney. It was oriented toward extreme sports, and she was able to pick up not only a tough and durable compression body suit but also some low-profile climbing shoes and gloves. She could keep these in a bag or pocket, to access them quickly.

She also purchased a few odds and ends for climbing, which could serve double duty as needed.

She wasn't prone to carrying a lot of gear with her when she was on a job, but the close calls had made it a necessity. She could still rely on what her grandfather had called "resource thinking," always keeping an inventory of what was around her, mentally cataloging what could be useful. She was simply stacking the deck a little.

It was worth the inconvenience.

Her final purchase was equal parts resource and nostalgia, however.

In a store window just down the block from the fitness store, she spotted a display of Swiss Army knives. She'd long since lost the one her grandfather had left her, which was some-thing she regretted keenly.

Letting it go had been necessary, though, and she would do it again, no question. But seeing the array of little red knives on a slowly rotating window display brought her right back to her childhood. She remembered sitting with her grandfather under a tree by a river, fishing poles nearby, as the two of them whit-tled sticks into sharpened spits they would use for roasting fish and marshmallows alike, later that evening.

She had cut herself badly on that trip and had screamed and cried all the while that Papa was cleaning and bandaging the wound.

"Why do you think you cut yourself?" he had asked her.

She sniffled and shook her head.

"It was because of one thing," he said, cupping her chin with one hand and looking into her eyes. "You didn't keep your mind on what you were doing." He smiled and let his hand drop away. "I taught you how to whittle. What were the rules I told you?"

She sniffled and said, "Pay attention."

"That's one. What was the other?"

She thought, sniffled some more, and looked down.

He tilted her head up. "Alex, sweet girl. It's ok. But when you realize you've made a mistake, you need to own up to it," he said. "You only get better at things when you're responsible for them. That means you have to admit when you did something wrong. Now, what did you do wrong? What was the second rule?"

She was crying, and it was hard to say the words when she looked up, her chin quivering. "I was s'posed to cut away from me," she said.

"Did you do that?" Papa asked.

She shook her head, tears flying away.

"So next time, what will you do?" he asked.

"I'll cut the other way," she said.

"And?"

She thought for a moment, then said, "I'll pay attention."

He smiled again, then raised her cut thumb. The bandage and Neosporin were keeping the blood where it belonged, but it hurt a lot.

Papa kissed her little hand, and somehow that made it better.

Standing on the sidewalk, looking in at the display of knives, Alex felt she could really use a kiss from her grandfather these days. Though some boo-boos were a little harder to kiss away than others.

She went inside and picked out a knife. This one was a bit bulkier than the one her grandfather had left her, but it came with an array of useful tools, including pliers and screwdrivers in multiple sizes. It had a good heft to it, too. It felt comforting to her, as if it contained the power to do anything she could imagine. Which really wasn't far from the truth.

The right tool in the right hands could do practically anything.

After leaving the store, she wandered down the way to a cafe, slipping into a booth with a view of the door and easy access to the rear exit. She made sure she was oriented so that she could spring up and away at an instant's notice, without being encumbered by the table's legs. She had her purchases consolidated into something easy to grab on the run, though she'd sacrifice them if she had to. The pocket knife was tucked into her pocket, though. That would definitely go with her.

It had been awhile since she'd been this paranoid in public, but it seemed warranted. She'd become a little too complacent. Maybe the close calls were a good thing, making her refocus and pay attention. She'd call them slips, tiny cuts that came with lessons. She could almost hear Papa's voice, telling her to keep her mind on what she was doing. And on who she was here for.

Abbey Cooper.

Alex had taken on this case because it had drifted to the bottom of the FBI's list of priorities, like detritus settling to the bottom of a lake. Maybe, someday, things would loosen up enough on the world stage that the FBI or the police or someone would get around to looking at Abbey's file again. It didn't feel likely. And in the meantime Abbey continued to suffer because of this. No one was stepping up to make it right.

So it was up to Alex.

But there were *so many damned questions.*

Worse, Alex realized as she sipped iced tea and nibbled at a chicken salad sandwich, there were *too many assumptions.*

First, Alex had assumed that the theft was motivated by the technology of the arm itself. Some of that technology and the software involved in its creation was classified, after all. Abbey was getting a special exception to have it for everyday use, simply because it was ultimately a dumbed down version of a more advanced prosthetic, and Uconic was ultimately looking to market it to the public, down the road.

What if that wasn't the reason it was stolen?

Her investigation into Uconic, and then Shorelite, had made at least one thing clear: Neither company was trying to hide anything beyond what they were legally obligated to hide.

Alex had now met the CEOs of both companies. She'd looked into them extensively, but meeting them face to face had given her a chance to use her intuition. And from what she could determine, neither of these men was harboring any sort of dark agenda. In fact, both had shown a capacity for concern, empathy, even kindness.

Tim Davis had seemly even kept his word and said nothing

to the FBI about Abbey Cooper. Alex used QuIEK to peek at the reports from yesterday's disaster, and there'd been no mention.

Not a guarantee. Agent Symon was the kind of guy who might catch on that Alex had an inside track into the FBI's investigation into her. He might have opted to keep that detail off the books.

Gauging by what was *on* the books, however, Alex didn't think so. Reading over reports from the past few days, she saw that Symon had taken a beating from his supervisors, over losing her at the park. And Agent Mayher—Tank Top, as Alex thought of her—had gotten a reprimand for discharging her firearm while in pursuit.

Alex rubbed her eyes, leaning back against the cushioned seat of the booth. The waiter came by to ask if she needed anything, and offered to refill her tea. She smiled, asked for the check, and turned to stare out of the window when he left.

Assumptions.

She shook her headhead suddenly realized the mistake she'd made.

This was too similar to what had happened to her at Populus.

Two tech firms, both with government contracts, and their technologies intended to help everyday people. But the government and military were calling dibs and decreasing the likelihood of these technologies ever being used for their intended purpose. Worse, the tech would be weaponized.

Two very different types of technology, but the same general outcome.

Alex could have smacked herself for being so obtuse.

These were windmills.

She was playing out her role of Don Quixote, tilting her

lance toward windmills that reminded her of the dragons of her past.

She'd seen those two technology firms as being part of the threat because she'd *wanted* them to be. She was working from an assumption, rather than working from facts.

And the facts were that the arm had been stolen, a young girl was the victim, and the motives were unclear or just simply unknown.

She needed to stop looking to support her assumptions and cognitive bias and start looking for missing bullet holes.

In World War II, the US had enlisted a number of scientists and mathematicians to help solve a laundry list of problems, to keep the US ahead of their enemies. The Nazis were employing scientists to speed up the creation of weapons and machines of war, and the US would do no less. To that end, the military turned to Abraham Wald.

Wald was a world-class mathematician, as well as a Jewish refugee fleeing from Nazi Germany. He was recruited into the Statistical Research Group—an unlikely but potent piece of the US war machinery, and one of its best resources.

The military came to Wald with a problem. They needed to improve the odds of their aircraft surviving air battles. The problem, as they framed it, was that they needed to find the ultimate balance between armor plating and fuel ratios.

More armor meant better protection, but it also meant making the aircraft heavier. Which meant burning through fuel faster, making the aircraft slower in air, and essentially reducing its effectiveness.

Less armor helped maximize fuel, agility, and speed, but it also made both the planes and the pilots more vulnerable.

The military brought Wald reams of data to work with, including data about the average number and location of bullet holes in the planes that survived. They gave him access to schematics and designs, with expert guidance on the most crucial and vulnerable parts of the planes.

The hope was that this data would allow Wald to figure the best configuration of armor plating—where to place it, and how much to use—reducing the chances that the planes were shot down while increasing fuel efficiency and maneuverability.

An odd anomaly, however, was that on average the data showed there were no bullet holes in the engine section of the plane.

The holes were spread more or less evenly around the rest of the fuselage, the wings, the tail, the cockpit. But the engine rarely had bullet holes.

Wald accepted the data, but his report wasn't what the military had expected or asked for.

Instead of recommendations for armor placement where the planes were taking the most hits, Wald recommended increasing armor only around the engines.

The military had made a false assumption, he explained. They had assumed that the data indicated vulnerabilities in the surviving aircraft. What it actually indicated was a vulnerability in the aircraft that had been shot down.

The reason there were no bullet holes in the engines of the surviving planes was because the planes that had taken bullet damage there had been shot down.

Wald's recommendation turned the tide and made American and British air power far more effective. More planes were saved, more pilots survived, and the odds were stacked much more in favor of the Allies.

Alex had always found this story both amusing and inspiring. It was the kind of story her grandfather would have smiled and nodded over. As an engineer and inventor himself, he knew that assumptions usually led to more work—typically the wrong work—and you would usually have to go back and start over, ignore the assumption and repair any damage you'd already done.

Alex had made a number of assumptions since arriving in Orlando, and they were making things very difficult.

She had to start back at zero.

Why would someone steal Abbey Cooper's arm?

Maybe it wasn't the arm itself, she suddenly realized.

Maybe it was Abbey Cooper.

CHAPTER THIRTEEN

"Run through it again," Symon said.

Mayher sat across from him, looking miserable.

He'd chosen to do this debrief at a coffee shop. It saved them some time driving back to HQ, but if he was being honest, it was also a more comfortable and inviting place to have a fairly serious talk.

"Kayne had distracted the police officers on scene, after taking out the local security guard and the CEO. When you and I saw her outside the building we split up, without waiting for other agents to arrive on scene. Your order was to track her and observe, but not to engage."

"You went into the facility and I went around outside, checking the perimeter. I was just rounding to the back of the facility when I saw Alex Kayne exit through the bay door. She was running to the fence."

"I ran toward her and drew my weapon and ordered her to get on the ground. She ignored my order and started to go over the fence. That's... when I fired."

"And what was your intention in discharging your weapon?" Symon asked.

Mayher sighed and shrugged. "A warning shot?" She shook her head. "I know that everything I did was against protocol, and your orders."

She slid the cup of coffee to one side and then back again. A fidgeting habit, Symon thought.

He studied her for a moment longer, then sipped his own coffee, thinking. "Julia... off the record. What were you thinking?"

She looked up and met his gaze. She was silent for a moment, then sighed heavily and shook her head. "I can't say for sure. It's just... I had this impulse. I *had* to make her stop. She just... she does these crazy things. She just keeps running. Getting away. Something in me just wanted to... I don't know. Get her attention."

Symon considered this, then nodded. "She's getting to you."

Mayher shook her head. "No. She's not. It's just that I've seen her file, read the reports from the agents who've been chasing her. She's smart. She's resourceful. She's managed to stay ahead of us for *two years*, and the whole time she's played this game, to show us how clever she is."

"Do you think that's what she's doing?" Symon asked. "She's showing off? She wants us to know she's smarter than we are?"

Mayher looked up, her turn to study him.

After a moment she shook her head, her expression miserable. "No," she said. "I don't know what her game is, and I think that's rattling me."

Symon sipped again from his coffee, then put the cup down. He leaned forward slightly, resting on his elbows. "Do you know why I asked for you to be assigned to this case with me?"

She smiled. "My indomitable charm?"

He smiled back, shaking his head. "You're the right combination of smart and tough. I've studied your sheet, Agent Mayher. You came through Quantico like you had something to prove, but you were also just flat-out the best in your class. Sharp. Resilient. Able to think down a crisis rather than being swept up in it. So you can understand why I'm surprised and concerned over how this went down today."

Mayher sat silent, watching, then nodded. "You're right. I acted out of character. On impulse. And worse, I disobeyed a direct order and possibly endangered people." She sighed and slumped a bit in her chair.

"I should be pulled from this case."

Symon barked a laugh and leaned back. He took up the coffee cup again. "Don't be ridiculous. It'd be more productive to replace myself than you. No, you made a decision based on your assessment of the situation. You perceived a potential threat, based on the suspect's actions, which included an assault on building security."

Mayher listened to this and blinked. "That's... a generous interpretation of events," she replied.

"Do you dispute it?" Symon asked.

Mayher paused, then shook her head.

"And as for future orders?"

Mayher leaned forward, letting her intensity show, "I follow orders," she said with great severity.

Symon smiled and nodded, then picked up the pen he had laid on the stack of forms shoved to one side of the table. He made a few quick notes, then signed the form before sliding it and the pen over to Mayher.

She read through it quickly, glancing up with slight

surprise only once, then signed the space above Symon's signature.

"So, consider this a minor reprimand. Given the immediacy of events, and the suspects history, not to mention her actions just prior to our arrival, you used your best judgement in discharging your weapon. And you've adequately demonstrated that you thought there could be an immediate threat. You did the best you could, under the circumstances. I commend you on your diligence, Agent Mayher."

He was giving her a hard look, the message and meaning clear.

No more chances on this. Orders would be followed from here out. He was in charge.

Mayher nodded, looking slightly relieved.

The truth was, Symon had no intention of putting a full reprimand in her file over this. He knew she hadn't intentionally disobeyed him. The discharge wasn't an unheard-of event in scenarios such as these, and he could spin things any way necessary to justify it.

The problem was Alex Kayne.

Once again, Kayne had managed to elude them at the last second. It was a little humiliating, but not altogether unexpected, based on her record.

She really was good. And apparently she'd spent the past two years making sure she got even better. The parkour moves, the Krav Maga and Ju Jitsu fighting styles—these weren't in her record. It was possible she'd studied these things prior to going on the run, but if anything it was obvious, she'd kept up her training. It made her even more dangerous and elusive.

Symon dismissed Mayher, telling her to meet him back at the office later. He lingered at the coffee shop, updating both Mayher's personnel file and the file on Alex Kayne. He noted her martial arts proficiency, intending to look into that further at some point. If she was still training, maybe this could be a lead. He'd check martial arts schools in the various cities where she'd been spotted. Same with any gyms that taught parkour.

For now, he turned his attention to her target.

After questioning Tim Davis and his security chief, along with the receptionist and a few others who had witnessed Kayne's escape, Symon had dug in a bit into what Shorelite Robotics was all about. It didn't take long to uncover their connection to Uconic Prosthetics. Davis had also given him access to the secure room that Kayne had managed to break into.

After referencing his notes and making some calls for confirmation, Symon had found some crossover.

The Uconic Unity Prosthetic—a sort of adaptive prosthetic technology that was just starting to trickle down to the public after being put to work for the US military.

It was impressive technology, and Symon deeply respected its purpose. He'd known a lot of good people who had ended up in need of a replacement limb, whether as a result of combat or just the unfortunate outcome of an accident. Regaining mobility and autonomy, Symon knew, was no small gift.

But what was Alex Kayne's interest in it, exactly?

She hadn't stolen anything from Shorelite. She'd merely gained access to a secure area. More or less a records vault.

Data gathering, then? Intel? But to what end?

Kayne's behavior was bizarre. She remained elusive, but even when her pursuers were close she lingered. It was as if she were waiting for something to run its course.

Or to finish something.

Symon leaned back, slowly raising his coffee to his lips, considering.

Kayne was a humanitarian. The work she'd done at Populus had been intended to benefit humanity. The papers she'd written, the social media and blog posts she'd shared, the collection of books she kept in her home and the tabs that had been open on her office computer—all of it painted a picture of Alex Kayne as being a concerned benefactor of humanity.

None of it gelled well with the idea that she was a rogue Russian operative, and a murderer.

The original profiler on this case had labeled all of this humanitarian effort as self aggrandizement. A hero complex, they said, indicating that she saw her alleged treason as being somehow noble. They had painted Kayne as being a delusional sociopath, with designs to become a beloved historic figure. She was depicted as a Guy Fawkes wannabe, essentially.

Symon saw her in a completely different way.

She'd been a philanthropist, but even before she'd achieved anything in business or had any significant money, she'd had a history of helping the little guy. She'd volunteered for organizations such as Habitat for Humanity. She'd been a Big Sister. She'd organized community outreach programs, helping people in impoverished areas to learn skills and trades—particularly skills that let them continue to improve their lives and communities after the programs ended.

Kayne had also helped to found a number of maker spaces in her own community—small groups that encouraged members to build and explore technology, to share skills and learn from each other. Kayne had bought a couple of abandoned buildings in the area, paid to have them renovated, and then donated them to these groups, free of charge, without so much as her name on a plague somewhere.

Alex Kayne had a fetish for encouraging resourcefulness, Symon determined. And she had a drive to help people who were powerless, or at the very least to help people who *saw* themselves as powerless. Everything he uncovered about her spoke volumes about a passion to empower others.

Hardly the work of a sociopath.

Maybe there really was some undercurrent of narcissism or self aggrandizement driving what she'd been doing prior to going on the run, but Symon doubted it. It seemed a lot more likely that she genuinely cared about people and wanted to help.

And why should that change, just because she was a fugitive?

The near-misses, the lingering and relocating locally, rather than going back on the run, the repeated intrusions into secure areas that could only jeopardize her further...

Alex Kayne had a mission.

Symon took out his phone and opened a browser. He started searching news sites, looking for any mention of Uconic, prosthetics, and particularly the UUP program. There were plenty of articles discussing the future of prosthetic design, and Uconic's role in that future. There were profiles on the founders, company backgrounds, celebrity appearances at public events.

Symon refined the search to crime reports, and the results were narrowed significantly.

Abbey Cooper.

There were hundreds of articles outlining the theft of her prosthetic arm, a UUP8 prototype that had been stolen from her apartment, even while she'd just been in the next room.

There was an air of tantalizing mystery about the articles, and a bit of shade cast on Abbey Cooper herself, at times. The media could be vicious when they thought they had something that would grab readers. Tearing down a girl who had just lost her arm, for the second time, was apparently not too much of a line to skirt, and to occasionally hopscotch over.

Symon had had his fair share of bad press and unwarranted suspicion, after Director Crispen had been taken into custody. It was the first time in his life that he'd been cast as the bad guy, and unfairly and unduly at that. It hadn't been pleasant, and he could admit he still held a bit of a grudge against the media.

That was the past, though. He tried to only revisit the past when he could mine it for data, to help with whatever puzzle he was working on in the present. Lingering too long on old wounds tended to reopen them.

He shook himself, letting a momentary wave of resentment pass like water off of his back. He had a job to do.

Symon continued studying news reports, and noted that not only had the police become involved in the Abbey Cooper case, the FBI had as well. The classified nature of some of the related technology had given the theft a much higher profile.

He logged onto the FBI's remote servers and pulled up the case file, noting that it hadn't seen much attention for several months. The case had gone cold and had more or less been deprioritized. It was still active, but no one had looked at it for quite some time.

No one, Symon realized, *but Alex Kayne.*

Reading through the reports, studying the investigation as it had progressed from the initial calls to the point where leads had fallen away and it had grown cold, Symon was struck by certain similarities to Kayne's own history.

Uconic's technology was something revolutionary, with implications and applications well beyond the public sector. As such, it had come to the attention of the US government and US military, who had designs on it that were not entirely friendly to civilian use.

Just as had happened with Populus, Uconic had signed contracts giving the US government broad control over the patents for the underlying technology. And while Uconic still publicly proclaimed that the tech was intended to help anyone who needed it, the reality was that a lot of their intellectual property was tied up in military applications.

It would be decades before the UUP tech was commercially available.

Just like that software that Alex Kayne had invented.

What was it called?

He checked Kayne's file and found it. Quantum Integrated Encryption Key. QuIEK for short. The file noted that the colloquial pronunciation was "quake," which made Symon smile.

Given how much Alexa Kayne had shaken things up for the FBI, the named seemed more than appropriate. And the more he studied the files on it, the more appropriate the name became.

It was more than just software. It was practically a super power.

QuIEK was the most advanced hacking tool on the planet, as far as Symon could tell. He couldn't even pretend to comprehend the details of it, but he knew enough to recognize exactly why the US and Russian governments would go to extremes to get it.

One section in the report stood out:

THE POTENTIAL DANGER *of QuIEK falling into the hands of foreign operatives cannot be overstated. This technology is lightweight, requiring next to nothing in terms of storage capacity or computer processing power. It could run as easily on a pocket calculator as on a NASA mainframe. But its capabilities are immeasurable.*

Using QuIEK, any foreign operative could access and infiltrate any computer system on the planet, including the most secure servers of the US government. Barring extreme measures, including air-gapped computer systems, there would be no way to prevent intrusion into even the most sensitive data. Even isolated systems would be accessible, if the operative could have physical access to them.

In short, QuIEk is the most powerful and most dangerous technology on the planet. Its retrieval should be the top priority of US law enforcement.

SYMON READ through the passage several times, taking in everything he understood. He scanned over the more technical documentation, but quickly abandoned trying to understand it. Everything started dipping into subjects such as quantum theory and mathematics at a level that would give Einstein a headache.

There was nothing in Kayne's file about her being a mathematics genius. She'd been a programmer, and had done some work at various physics laboratories worldwide, but she was no physicist herself.

By all accounts, she'd done something miraculous—cobbling together the world's most advanced software by trial and error, and a lot of instinct.

It spoke volumes about Kayne herself, in Symon's estimate.

For a start, she was a lot smarter than they'd even given her credit for. Her ability to think ahead, to visualize things in multiple dimensions, with a sort of grassroots practicality tinged with genius-level strategic thinking...

It was no wonder she kept eluding them. It was a miracle they'd even gotten as close to her as they had.

Because, Symon now realized, she had more than her smarts as an advantage.

The file said that Kayne had destroyed QuIEK. Or rather, that she had locked it up tight within the servers of Populus. Servers that were currently residing in an undisclosed location, being picked at by the smartest tech guys on the planet. They were working day and night, using the most advanced equipment the US government could provide, to try to crack QuIEK's encryption and reclaim QuIEK itself.

Based on what he was reading, however, Symon realized they were wasting their time.

Not only would they never retrieve the software, without the software itself, they were also looking in the wrong place.

It could run as easily on a pocket calculator as on a NASA mainframe.

Or on a mobile phone.

There was footage from Shorelite on his computer, and he brought this up, scanning through it to track Kayne as she'd moved through the facility. He stopped each time she passed through any sort of security checkpoint.

There it was.

She used her phone every time.

Thumbprint scanners, security badge readers, whatever, she had her phone close by just as she gained access.

She was running QuIEK. No digital system could stop her. She could walk through, like it wasn't even there.

Which meant it could easily give Kayne access to the FBI case files.

Everything regarding both Kayne's case and the Abbey Cooper case was on the FBI's servers. Any time Kayne wanted, she could use her super power to take a look, to get up to speed, and to outmaneuver the FBI at every turn.

Symon wasn't foolish enough to think this was the *only* reason she stayed ahead of them. But it certainly gave her some big advantages.

He leaned back, then snagged the coffee cup again, sipping, putting it down. He stared at his screen, thinking.

The profile on Alex Kayne was wrong. As far as it went, at least, it was wrong. Its conclusions, also, were wrong.

Alex Kayne really was the altruistic person she appeared to be. And she was certainly not working for the Russians.

She was helping people.

People like Abbey Cooper.

With her propensity toward helping the downtrodden and disenfranchised, she would be drawn like a moth to this particular flame. A young girl, the victim of a tragic and traumatic event, further slighted by the theft of something that had given her a new hope.

And the FBI, having found *nothing*—had essentially given up on Abbey Cooper, while doggedly pursuing Alex Kayne, who saw herself as innocent as well.

The pieces clicked together like magnets, and Symon saw it all clearly for the first time.

Alex Kayne was here for Abbey Cooper. She was here to right a wrong, to bring justice to a forgotten case.

Symon went back to Kayne's file, then spent more time sifting through the FBI database and various news sites. There had been a number of close calls over the past two years, but they'd been written off as the inevitable sort of slips that fugitives made. Everyone slips up, was the philosophy. Everyone makes a mistake that will, eventually, land them in handcuffs. It was typical for fugitives to screw up, eventually—some profilers even believed it was subconsciously intentional. They *wanted* to be caught, and so they made mistakes.

The reports completely discounted a fact that Symon now knew for certain:

Alex Kayne was not a typical fugitive.

If she had decided to disappear, to remain hidden for the rest of her life, she could have done it easily. She still could. With QuIEK, she had zero reason to even stay in the country.

She could reinvent herself somewhere with no extradition treaty and have offshore bank accounts crammed with money to see her through until the end of her days.

Alex Kayne did not have to run.

She chose to.

For whatever reason, thanks to some quirk of her psychology maybe, she was immune to the typical mistakes that fugitives made. She never reached out to old acquaintances. She never tried to rebuild her former life. She never seemed to care about the progress the FBI was making in the manhunt—though Symon now realized she could pick up every detail of the case without leaving so much as a hint that she'd been in the system.

Kayne was definitely on the run, but she was also on a mission. The reason they would occasionally find traces of her, and even come close to catching her, was because she refused to abandon whatever mission she was on, from city to city. She was there to help someone, and she wouldn't leave until the job was done.

It was like some sort of personal rule, Symon realized. She had a code.

And here, in Orlando, she was on a mission to find and return Abbey Cooper's prosthetic arm. She was here to bring justice for Abbey.

And the mission wasn't over yet.

Symon closed Kayne's file, and slipped his phone back into the inner pocket of his coat. He took a last sip of the coffee, and then stood, making his way outside to his car.

He knew he had just cracked this case.

He knew, now, how to find Alex Kayne.

It was time to bring her in.

He just wasn't sure how he felt about it.

CHAPTER FOURTEEN

ALEX HAD A BAD FEELING.

She wasn't much of a believer in psychic phenomenon, but she was a true believer when it came to intuition and gut instinct. She'd long ago decided that intuition was the result of her subconscious sifting through all the data it was receiving, noticing things she might not be consciously aware of, and making logical leaps that were often highly accurate.

A lifetime of "resource thinking" had helped to hone this, and she had come to be perfectly comfortable trusting her gut feelings. In the absence of any other information, her intuition was the best source she had for making decisions.

Right now her intuition was telling her to keep her distance.

She'd only met with Abbey Cooper once, in person, and prior to that she'd exchanged a series of text messages with her. Using QuIEK, Alex had been able to originate those messages from a variety of spoofed numbers, relayed via a free VoIP phone number.

Even with a trap number, such as what skip tracers and PIs

used, there was no way to trace any of the messages back to Alex. She could keep them running in circles for eternity.

But it hardly mattered. Thanks to Smokescreen, even if someone did manage to trace through all the tangles and loop backs, they'd tend to go looking for her in some remote part of the country, hundreds or even thousands of miles from where she actually was.

Alex had done her research on Abbey, just as she had with all of her clients. She knew the girl as well as anyone could know her, if they weren't personally involved in her life. All the data was there, from her social media presence to her driving record to her preference of pizza toppings. Her school records indicated she was smart and a hard worker. Her thesis had shown some real insight, though it was a little soft on details. And there were plenty of news stories about her, as a result of the shark attack as well as receiving her prosthetic arm, not to mention the theft of that arm. Some of those stories were hit pieces, which was a little sickening to read. But they contributed details that Alex was able to parse and vet, and a lot of it checked out.

There was a great deal that Alex could know about Abbey based on her digital footprint.

But none of that had hinted at why someone would target *her*, specifically, and steal the arm.

Alex continued to look closer at Abbey's overall profile. If there were hints there, she'd find them, eventually. Intuitive leaps would win the day, even if Alex wasn't seeing much on the surface.

But that sort of thing took time. And distraction. Alex had to let her mind mull things over, so synapses could link and random ideas could gel into legitimate solutions.

Soon.

At the moment Alex was observing Abbey IRL—in real life.

It was a rare thing for Alex to circle back around on the client. She'd always tried to keep her distance, out of a sense of self-preservation if for no other reason. The client was the reason she was in any given place and staying away meant that the FBI would have less opportunity to uncover her motives for being there. Distance, while she worked, meant security.

There was still something to be said, though, for examining how someone behaved in the three-dimensional world. If someone in Abbey's life was behind this, Alex's best chance of finding them was to watch Abbey's personal interactions, and be alert for clues and leads. There was no real harm in it, if she kept her distance.

But Alex's Spidey sense was definitely tingling.

Something wasn't right. Or something was wrong. The two concepts had different implications, depending on the context. Either way, her instincts were telling her that being out in the open right now was a bad idea.

For the moment she'd stay out of sight, hanging back at the fringes. She needed more information, but she also needed to keep herself out of a prison cell long enough to help Abbey Cooper.

At the moment, Alex was sitting in a Starbucks close to Abbey's apartment. She had a tablet propped in front of her and had used Smokescreen and QuIEK to tap into a series of local traffic and ATM cameras. From this spot she could see every entrance and exit of the apartment building where Abbey lived with her roommate. And when she saw Abbey leave, she tracked her, camera by camera, for the three blocks she walked to get to her job.

Maritef, a marine ecology consulting group, was actually a Fiji-based organization that provided EIAs—Environmental

Impact Assessments. The US branch typically focused on environmentally catastrophic events in the Gulf of Mexico, where a number of major oil spills had impacted marine ecology.

According to her personnel file, Abbey was part of the marine biology team, which made sense. There were a number of personal notes in her file, from her supervisor and her teammates. Despite missing an arm, it was clear that Abbey was a determined and capable member of her team. Her performance reviews read like a recommendation for a medal.

Alex broadened her search of Maritef's database, looking for anything that might hint at some sort of animosity toward her, maybe from one of her teammates.

But there was nothing. Everyone loved her.

Next Alex looked deeper into the company itself.

The Fiji-based consulting group was formed in response to increasing demand for resources to help assess and mitigate the impact of pollutants in the world's oceans. Since the late nineties, Maritef had worked to create awareness programs through marine tourism, as well as ecological protection and repair programs through scientific research.

The firm had done a remarkable job, too. It had aided in the rescue of sea life numbering in the thousands during such catastrophes as the Deep Water Horizon spill, and its eco-tourism efforts were popular in regions like Florida. The value of promoting awareness was hard to measure, but Alex suspected it was enough to move the needle at least a bit.

The research at Maritef was not limited to marine biology, of course. They were heavily involved in the development of new technologies, aimed at both exploration and intervention. This involvement usually came in the form of contributions to research, to strategic partners. Maritef had hands-on experience with local marine life and ecologies in various parts of the world, and their insight was valuable.

Strategic partners.

That might be a lead.

Alex dove into this, looking through all the public and private relationships that Maritef had established. But it turned into a dead end.

Maritef did have numerous benefactors and partnerships, including Uconic. This was no coincidence, however. Uconic had become a sponsor of Maritef's aquatic robotics program as a result of Abbey Cooper's employment with the firm. She was the bridge connecting the two.

And as far as Alex could determine, none of Maritef's programs or technologies incorporated anything that raised a red flag. Uconic's contributions were largely financial, but they also supplied a great deal of technology—all of which was essentially "middle shelf."

There would really be no need for anyone at Maritef to steal the UUP8 prototype, as far as Alex could determine. They already had access to a host of Uconic technologies that would aid in their research. It was good publicity for Uconic, and a good source of funding and technological advancement for Maritef. Everyone came out a winner, thanks to Abbey Cooper.

So who was *not* coming out a winner?

Good question. Frustrating question.

The trouble with this case, unlike most of the cases Alex had undertaken over the past two years, was there was no sign of a motive. Everyone she'd looked into so far had actually turned out to be one of the good guys. No one had any reason to take the UUP8 prototype—in fact, they had every reason to want Abbey Cooper to keep using it.

Things were at a dead end. Again.

Worse, because she'd make some mistakes and gotten sloppy, Alex was dealing with not only a lack of forward momentum in this case but also the looming threat of the FBI nabbing her at any minute. She was starting to reconsider her policy of never leaving a job unfinished.

As usual, though, she could almost feel her grandfather giving her a disappointing look.

When you take something on, that makes it worth finishing.

This kind of thinking had driven Alex nuts plenty of times over the years, but it had made her far more cautious about the things she committed to. Unlike her friends in college, Alex never had a stack of half-read books or abandoned knitting projects. When she took something on, she was absolutely committed to finishing it, no matter how dreadful the experience turned out to be.

This was how she'd created QuIEK, despite having very little experience in programming or quantum mechanics. When she'd decided to dip a toe into those waters, she'd just gone ahead and plunged in. Full immersion. And even when she was pulling her hair out trying to solve some of the stickier problems of creating, essentially, the world's most advanced digital security software, she couldn't walk away from it. She had to stay in it until it was done, or die trying.

Some values were too engrained.

A job started is a responsibility and a commitment, her Papa would remind her. Probably in a much more folksy way. But always with that edge of common sense mingled with self-empowered pride that simply *was* her grandfather.

She couldn't let him down.

She couldn't let Abbey Cooper down.

She stood and stretched, looking around the Starbucks, taking it in as a means of mental distraction.

Things were a little slow here, which was fine by her. Only a handful of people had entered since she'd arrived, and none had stayed long. The same four people who had been seated when she came in were scattered around the space, using laptops or reading newspapers or simply chatting with each other. Two old timers had taken up a table near her and were discussing the baseball game from the previous night, as well as their dismal scores on the golf course.

Everything was fine. But her gut was still nagging her. It was time to go.

She didn't have to be in proximity to Abbey to track her, now that she had her general environment mapped out. In fact, hanging too close would be dangerous. Alex needed to avoid anything that put her in a predictable location at a predictable time. Agent Symon was sure to uncover the common link between Uconic and Shorelite at some point. He was too smart to miss it. And from there, it wasn't much of a leap to get to Abbey Cooper.

It was how Alex would have done it.

Another pearl of wisdom from Papa floated to the surface.

Assume everyone is smarter than you are and no one will ever take you by surprise.

It was good advice. It worked in every aspect of her life. It had helped her in business and in personal relationships. If she assumed everyone knew more than she did, then she was forced to keep thinking of new and alternative possibilities. She knew she was smart, so in a way this was Alex trying to out-think Alex. But the result was a lack of complacency that helped her keep an edge, and to stay ahead as much as possible.

If she assumed the FBI was onto her, she would have to keep sharp all the time, to stop making stupid mistakes, and to start doing things the right way. That was how she'd recover from her screwups, and how she'd get things back on track.

She slipped the smart tablet into her shoulder bag and left the Starbucks, pulling on a sunhat and large sunglasses as she stepped out into the bright Orlando day. She was in the role of a wealthy housewife today and had rented a car that matched the part—a little red convertible sat in a space just out front. Alex slipped into it, tossing her bag into the passenger seat.

She had her hair in a pony tail, the extensions giving it some length, and she was wearing a sun dress that revealed her shoulders. Beneath the outfit, however, she was wearing tight-fitting running clothes. It was a bit warm, and she could feel the sweat tricking down her side, but if she ended up having to make a fast exit, the discomfort would be worth it.

She left the Starbucks and drove the car back to the rental lot, calling for an Uber while she was still driving.

She was just about to turn into the lot when she saw her.

She'd come into the Starbucks earlier, had ordered something and left without so much as glancing Alex's way. As nondescript a transaction as possible, and if Alex hadn't been so committed to maintaining a state of deep paranoia, she might not have noticed her.

Now, here she was, the car behind. Alex recognized her despite the sunglasses.

There was a light, and Alex stopped. She was able to glance at the rearview mirror without moving her head, and without signaling with her eyes, thanks to the large sunglasses. She studied the face of the woman behind her and tried to determine if there was anything about her that indicated her intent.

She seemed very casual, and Alex was the first to admit she wasn't the world's best at reading body language.

Was it possible this was just a coincidence? Maybe the woman lived nearby and was running errands. Alex could be reading too much into it.

But then there was her intuition.

When the light changed Alex accelerated at an even pace, pushing her speed slightly and watching to see if the woman did anything unusual. So far, there was nothing.

The car rental place was coming up on Alex's right. The Uber app had just pinged her to say it was waiting. All Alex would have to do was park and drop the keys in a lock box outside of the rental office, and climb into her Uber. But if she was being followed, that was the last thing she intended to do.

She passed the rental office and picked up her phone, tapping the screen.

The next bit was going to be tricky.

At the next light, Alex put her blinker on, then slowed almost to a stop before turning. She watched the mirror, and sure enough the woman turned as well, though she seemed to be keeping her distance.

Alex was about a block ahead, and as she entered a residential neighborhood, she once again put on a blinker, slowed, and turned.

This time, as soon as a house was between her and the woman, she jammed the accelerator to the floor, gunning it and racing ahead. As she came to the next street, she gave the wheel a hard turn. Her tires squealed as she fishtailed a bit, and she turned into the skid and righted herself immediately, keeping the accelerator down.

She spotted him up ahead.

She hit the brakes and turned into a driveway, turned off the engine and left the keys. She grabbed her bag and raced to the Uber, jumping in.

"Hi," she smiled, huffing a little. "Thanks for agreeing to meet me here."

"No problem," the man said. He started tapping the screen of his phone, which was mounted on the dash.

Alex took off the sun hat, and fished out her own phone, using its reflective screen to peer over the top of the back seat as she scooted down. She saw the woman's SUV turn the corner, moving a bit faster than before.

Things could go very wrong here, Alex knew. She changed positions and ducked down so that she was hidden by the driver-side rear door. The SUV slowed a bit as it passed, but otherwise kept moving.

The Uber driver pulled out and started driving. "If you would like to nap, please feel free," he said in a heavy accent.

"Thank you," Alex smiled. She started tapping her phone, making arrangements. This next part was going to be tricky and would take some quick planning, but she had prepared for something like this in advance.

She accessed Smokescreen and started things moving.

When she had everything in place, she slid up in the seat, looking around. The SUV was gone, but that might not mean anything. Any given vehicle could be backup and surveillance at this point.

She looked back to her phone and made some adjustments.

"That is strange," the driver said. "The route just updated." He looked back at her in the mirror. "It says to drop you off here."

She smiled. "This is where I was going. Maybe something went glitchy?"

He looked at her for a moment then shook his head, smiling. He pulled over and she climbed out, then immediately ducked into a bar nearby.

She raced through without stopping and pushed through the rear exit. She dumped her bag and the sun dress in the dumpster and pulled on a pair of running shoes. The sun hat was replaced by a ball cap, and the oversized sunglasses were replaced by sports goggles.

She unclipped the hair extensions and dropped those in the dumpster. She then pulled out an exercise arm band, tucking her phone into it and popping in a pair of wireless ear buds.

She started running full tilt then, at one point hurdling a

fence to cut through someone's yard and onto the street on the other side of the house.

She was a jogger now, out for a mid-day run.

No one seemed to be following her—no cars appeared to tail her, and the few people she saw on the street were elderly and typically showing no interest in her.

She cut through a few blocks, making an elaborate circuit through the neighborhood. She periodically stopped to check her phone, to realign the map in her head and to check on the other arrangements she'd made.

Several blocks later she abruptly stopped running and climbed into the backseat of another Uber.

There was a brief exchange, some pleasantries, and then the ride ended a couple of miles away. She climbed out and jogged to the next pickup point.

There was no way for the FBI to trace any of these movements, thanks to Smokescreen. From the perspective of Uber's systems, dozens of requests had been made from locations all over the city, and all of them would be registered as completed fares, with tips, by the time the day was done. For now, Alex had an endless number of pickup points to choose from, and she was swapping rides at irregular intervals.

In this way she got to the clothing store where she'd stashed one of her backpacks. She ducked into one of the changing booths and retrieved it from the ceiling, then took a moment to update her look.

When she left, she was a completely different person, for the third time that day.

The feeling in her gut subsided. She'd managed to evade her pursuers, though it had cost her most of the day.

That was alright. Another of her Papa's sayings came to mind.

You got nowhere to go and you're in no hurry to get there.

It was how he'd reminded her to stay sharp and focused, to not get in a hurry when she was learning to drive. Like most of Papa's pearls of wisdom, it worked for a variety of situations.

Nowhere to go. No rush to get there. Slow and steady wins the race.

Her heart was pounding out of control.

This was the third close call since she'd taken on this case. This time she'd prepared in advance, but it could just as easily have gone wrong. Still, her preparations had worked. She'd made it. She was safe.

That was somewhat validating.

But all of this was a distraction from Abbey's case. Trying to keep ahead of the FBI at the moment was becoming her full-time job, and that was a problem.

She saw no way around it.

Something would have to be done about Agent Eric Symon.

CHAPTER FIFTEEN

SYMON RE-WATCHED the dash cam footage, stopping it at the point where the agent had passed right by Alex Kayne. It had been 24 hours since this footage was recorded, which may as well have been a week.

Kayne was once again in the wind.

Symon didn't worry about it. There was pressure from above, and it was certainly frustrating to lose her again. And again. But what Symon knew, and his superiors would simply refuse to accept, was that every encounter gave them more data to work with. Every miss was unfortunate, but it was also informative.

He looked at the screen, studying it, working through it.

The residents in the home where she'd left the rental car had called to report a strange vehicle in their driveway. The rental agency was contacted, and confirmed that the convertible had been rented that day by a woman matching Alex Kayne's general description, and matching exactly the description his agent had given, after surveilling her at the Starbucks.

The problem was they hadn't been able to make a positive

ID. The agent had followed Kayne in hopes of doing just that, and the sudden chase had been a little unexpected.

It shouldn't have been.

One thing that was clear now was that Alex Kayne knew their playbook and was always working under the assumption that the FBI was close. She was alert, and she was resourceful. With QuIEK, she was practically clairvoyant.

She wasn't going to be taken down with the usual methods.

Symon was going to have to get creative.

Getting creative, however, was not something the FBI necessarily endorsed. Bureaucracy wasn't exactly known for encouraging individual expression. And working around the rules, as Symon knew too well, could get an agent into a lot of trouble, regardless of how good his track record might be.

He leaned in closer to the video. The man behind the wheel, an Uber driver they had already tracked down and interviewed, was no one in the case. He gave them as much information as he could. He had at first thought his fare would nap in the back seat. He had originally been taking her to a drop-off in downtown Orlando. His destination updated suddenly, in a bizarre and unusual way, and the woman got out after just a few blocks. She entered a bar. She had tipped big.

The bar was also a dead end. No one had noticed her enter or leave, and there was no working video surveillance. The woman's bag, along with her clothes and hair extensions, had been found in the dumpster out back. The bag contained a smart tablet, but the tech team had verified that it was wiped clean. "Surgically clean," one of the guys had told him, shaking his head in wonder and admiration.

Somehow Alex Kayne had recognized that an agent was following her, had managed to evade that agent, and had then disappeared. No trace. No leads. No chance.

It was the third time she'd gotten away from Symon and his

team, and his superiors had made it painfully clear that it had best be the last.

The waitress came by to grab his check and his credit card, disappearing through the door to the kitchen. Symon picked up the ceramic coffee cup by its rim, sipping one last time as he scrubbed through the video timeline once more. There was a brief blink from the laptop's screen, which made him pause, and then, abruptly, the screen went blank.

Symon tapped a few keys and moved his finger over the touch pad. Nothing. It seemed to be dead.

He picked his phone out of his coat pocket. He'd call tech and have them deliver a new laptop while this one was looked at. Everything was on the server, anyway. He could pick up where he'd left off.

He unlocked the phone and tapped the icon for his contacts. Instead of opening the contact app, however, the phone suddenly dialed an unknown number.

It was answered almost immediately, and he held the phone up to his ear, ready to apologize for misdialing.

"Hello Agent Symon," a woman's voice said from the other side.

Symon blinked. He'd never heard the voice before, but the confluence of details surrounding the call made things click immediately.

"Alex Kayne," he said.

"It's good to see you in something other than workout clothes. Wave to the camera for me," she said, her tone bright.

Symon looked up and scanned the line of the ceiling until he spotted the camera. "You're hacking into restaurant security now?" he replied wryly.

"You know, I don't actually consider myself a hacker. That term gets used a lot, and it's usually wrong. I was more of a programmer, maybe an amateur physicist, before all this started. QuIEK was less about gaining access to things and more about... well, securing them, honestly. But let's just say I'm not actually a hacker. The rest could get complicated."

"Oh, I know all about your background, Alex. I've studied everything there is about you."

"Then you know I'm innocent of collusion with the Russians," she said.

"Do I?"

"You couldn't possibly look that deeply into my life and think I'd ever do what I was accused of. I didn't kill Adrian. He was..." she paused, and Symon thought he could hear the emotion being held in check. "He was my friend. Even after he betrayed me. Kind of a shitty friend, but still."

"Yes, the file does say you tried to pin everything on Adrian Ballard." He was pushing, being deliberately confrontational, hoping to shake her up.

"I did," she said. "I gave that up, after it became clear that no one believed me."

"That's not true," Symon said. The waitress was returning with his check and credit card, a strange look on her face. "I do believe you're innocent of collusion and espionage," he said.

The waitress stood before him and the check and card on the table. "I'm sorry Mr. Symon, but your card was declined. But it's kind of ok... someone called and paid the bill anyway. My manager took the call and told me after I tried charging you."

Symon looked from her to the card and back again. "Ok," he said. "Sorry for the confusion."

She smiled at him and then left.

"You canceled my credit card?" Symon said into the phone, laughing lightly. "And you say you're not a hacker? Seems kind of petty."

"Actually, I canceled all of the FBI's credit cards," she said, and he could almost hear the smile in her voice. "It's kind of a bank error. It should be resolved in a few hours."

"You do realize that even if you're not guilty of espionage you're definitely guilty of about a hundred other crimes, right? Automotive theft, identity theft, credit card fraud... murder."

"The two Russian agents," she said calmly. "I did kill those two. Sort of a 'them or me' situation."

He let that linger before replying, "I can help with that one. We identified those agents at the time. They were in the country illegally and wanted worldwide for all sorts of nasty stuff. It would be easy to make that a self defense case. If you turn yourself in, I can make sure that charge is dropped. Everyone's pretty convinced you were being kidnapped, anyway. We found your car, and we saw video footage from the scene. To be honest, it's been discussed that we could drop the espionage charges too. If you cooperate."

"And by cooperate, you mean take off the lock the Populus servers and hand over QuIEK."

"That's right," Symon said. "I can't help you, Alex, if you don't turn over the government property you stole."

"Yeah, about that... I didn't sign anything saying the government owned my intellectual property."

"Your partner did, though."

"He did," she agreed. "He also conspired to hand it over to the Russians. It's a sticky mess, for sure. I don't expect I'll ever be untangled from it. And I don't expect I'll ever see life outside of a cell, if I turn myself in."

"It could happen," Symon said.

She laughed. "House arrest then. An ankle monitor. Restrictions on where I can go, and what technology I'm allowed to use. Yeah, I'm aware of the alternatives," she said. "Not in a million years."

She paused, only a beat, and said, "Agent Symon..."

"Call me Eric," he said.

"How personal," she replied. "Way to win my trust, Eric. Ok, listen, I came to grips with my... *situation*... almost two years ago. I tried to do this the right way. Or the FBI's way, at least. You've seen that in my file?"

"I know about the deal, and I know it was a trap. Bad faith bargaining. It's something I don't do. Or condone." He emphasized this last bit, hoping that it would win at least some trust from her.

"So you can understand why I'll never put myself in that position again, right?"

"All I can tell you is that you can trust me, Alex. And to be honest, you really don't have a choice. I'm going to find you, eventually. I'm going to bring you in. I'd rather do it on better terms than having you trussed up and carried in."

"I've looked at your file, too, Eric," Alex said. "You've had your own dust ups with the FBI. Some big trouble, too. Not all of it is settled, according to some files I've read."

Symon let that pass. He'd been more or less certain that was the case, but he would let Alex think she'd rattled him.

"I'm glad to see you were able to get past it and resume your career."

"I did my time. So to speak," Symon said. "My mistakes should actually prove to you that I can be trusted."

"They help," Alex agreed. "But it's really not about trust, Eric. I'm just not going to give up. Ever."

"Aren't you tired?" he asked, his tone now consolatory and quiet. "Alex, it's been *two years*. All that running. All that hiding. No personal relationships, no one to trust. Aren't you tired?"

"I take vacations," she said. "It's not so different from being the CEO of a technology company, really. Long hours, and the schedule can get brutal."

"Especially with a client list, right?" Eric asked.

For the first time, the pause on the other end of the phone seemed more like surprise than a calculated play of emotion.

He'd gotten a hit for once.

"I just wanted you to know that I have no intention of giving up, and that I'm annoyed enough with you and the FBI that I plan to start making things difficult."

He smiled. "You've already made things difficult, Alex. I had my ass handed to me for losing you for the third time in a row."

"Oh that?" she laughed. "That's a Tuesday for me. But you've cost me some time and set back my current... project. And that's something that really annoys me. So now I start annoying you back. I know it's not going to make you back off, but it'll be kind of cathartic for me."

"So, what, your strategy is to cancel credit cards and be a turd to the FBI?"

"For a start," she said. "Hang on to that phone. I can reach you pretty much any time, but the only way you can reach me is with this specific phone."

"Oh?" Symon asked. "Will I need to reach you?"

"You will," she said. "There's an app on your home screen now, called Alex. Just hit that and it'll call me."

"And I'm guessing I won't be able to trace that call," Symon said.

"You can trace it all you want," she replied, a smile in her voice. "Enjoy the trip."

With that she hung up, and the screen of Symon's laptop came back on. The video was still cued to the spot he'd been watching.

Everything was back to normal.

He packed everything away and went out to his car. This

little encounter with Alex Kayne hadn't rattled him. He'd more or less expected something like this to happen at some point.

He took it as a sign that they'd gotten too close, and they'd managed to get under her skin.

That was good. That could push her to make some mistakes. And mistakes were gold when hunting fugitives.

But more than that, Symon had managed to get a lead out of the conversation. One he was pretty sure Alex Kayne hadn't intended for him to pick up.

She had said that she took vacations, to combat the loneliness and stress of being on the run.

Symon started his car and put it into gear. He would stop by the FBI offices and grab a second phone. He'd keep this one for reaching Alex Kayne, but he didn't plan to make it simple for her to just monitor his calls and messages.

While he was at the office, he'd also pull together a team. He had a destination now. He knew where Alex Kayne was hiding out.

He was going to Disney World.

CHAPTER SIXTEEN

DID IT WORK?

Alex couldn't be entirely sure. She'd done her best to put a little fear of God into Agent Symon—*Eric*, she corrected. But he was an FBI agent, after all. In fact, he'd had a pretty impressive career, both before and after he started his time with the FBI. It was pretty clear he didn't scare easily.

But scaring him was only part of the strategy.

Either way, it was going to be awhile before she'd really know if everything worked as intended, if all the seeds would take root. And in the meantime, she had to leverage the window she'd opened for herself, to see if she could make some headway on Abbey's case.

It was time to start from ground zero and work her way outward.

There was a lot about this plan that made it dangerously stupid, but she was counting on Eric being a little preoccupied, and on the resources he was managing to be focused in a different place.

He had figured out the connection between Uconic and

Shorelite, which had led him and his team to Abbey Cooper. That was how they'd found Alex, though she was guessing they hadn't gotten a positive ID on her when she'd made a run for it. If they had, they would have surrounded that Starbucks, and she'd be sitting in a cell right now.

Instead, she was breaking and entering.

Abbey's roommate worked an afternoon shift at a clothing store several miles away. Abbey herself wouldn't leave work for a few hours. That meant the apartment was clear.

Alex used a bit of thin wire as a rake and a hairpin as a wrench, and in a short time she was able to pick the deadbolt and the door handle. It might have been her best time yet, but it was kind of a cheat. The deadbolt was mounted upside down and was maybe forty years old. Over time the springs had weakened and the pins became loose, making it easier to pick.

So, really, it didn't count.

Inside the apartment, Alex wasted no time. She setup the 360 camera, and started taking footage, moving the camera from room to room as she completed each sweep. She'd stitch all of this together later, in case she wanted to revisit the scene or take a closer look at anything—a handy way to take the scene with her, just in case.

She spent time snapping photos of every entrance and exit. It had been more than a year since the arm had been stolen, and both the police report and the FBI's files included photos and notes.

There had been no evidence of forced entry. Someone might have picked their way in just like Alex had, of course. But according to the reports, the deadbolt was still locked.

Maybe someone had a key.

The police had explored that angle, though. They had interviewed everyone Abbey knew who came anywhere near being a suspect, but everyone had been cleared. A few past tenants had been interviewed as well, as had the landlord, with the same results.

Nothing.

Alex stood in the middle of the living room, rotating slowly, taking everything in. She looked to her phone, at the crime scene photos the FBI had on file. Few things had changed since the day the arm had been stolen. The furniture, the art on the walls, even the arrangements of throw pillows were all the same. The magazines spread on the coffee table were different. There were different notes and reminders on the refrigerator. Beyond that, though, she may as well have been here on the day these shots were taken.

She went into Abbey's room and started to snoop.

According to the police report, Abbey kept the arm on top of the tall dresser just inside her bedroom door. It was plugged into a charging base, and Abbey had recalled seeing that charging light in the morning, shining steadily to indicate a full charge. It was her habit to make sure, since she'd accidentally left it off charge early on.

Alex stood by the dresser, then turned and looked through the bedroom door. From the bedroom to the front door was maybe eight paces. Not a tremendous leap. Someone could easily dash into the room and grab both the arm and its charger and make it out of the front door before Abbey could rinse the soap from her eyes.

Both Abbey and her roommate had confirmed that the door had been locked, both before and after the theft. Abbey was obsessive about locking the door. The roommate, Rachel West, confirmed Abbey's compulsive behavior.

Alex made her way to Rachel's room now.

She felt a bit more hesitant about this one. Abbey was her client, and there was a certain amount of assumed intrusiveness there. Rachel, on the other hand, had no idea who Alex was.

This whole thing was kind of sketchy anyway, but Alex really felt like she was crossing a line or two by entering Rachel's room.

Still, there was a job to do. And the police and FBI had both been far more intrusive than Alex intended to be.

She had looked into Rachel a bit, doing some background on her as part of a routine search. There wasn't anything altogether suspicious about her. She was a typical post-college girl trying to establish her independence. She had student loan debt, but nothing she couldn't manage with her current job and the benefits of having a roommate. She had a little credit card debt that probably wasn't wise, but she was paying this as well. And there were no medical bills or other debts to be found, for Rachel or any of her close family. Or her extended family, for that matter.

Alex found Rachel's laptop on a small table by the window. She used QuIEK to get into it and start sniffing around. She didn't want to waste too much time, so she loaded the same software she was using with her bots, and then set things up so that the files on Rachel's hard drive would index and mirror to a remote server. Alex could sort through all of it later, if she needed to.

After a while she finished up, breaking down the camera and tripod and stowing them in the shoulder bag she'd brought. She had the camera sync to Smokescreen via WiFi, as a backup, and she'd get to the footage later.

Alex sighed as she peeked out of the door's peep hole and then slipped quickly out into the hall.

Disappointing.

She hadn't found anything that put her any closer than she had been when she'd arrived. For all intents and purposes, this was a classic locked room mystery. Somehow, someone had broken in to a locked apartment without showing any signs of entry, stolen the arm just as Abbey had been in the shower, and then made their escape, locking the door behind them as they went, for reasons Alex couldn't begin to fathom.

Maybe Abbey did it.

On the surface, it didn't make much sense, but there could be any number of reasons why someone would make themselves the victim of a crime. Abbey had gotten quite a bit of attention after the loss of her arm, and again after receiving the prosthetic. Maybe she missed it. Maybe she valued that attention more than having her mobility back.

Stranger things had happened, Alex knew. And people who had suffered a severe psychological trauma would sometimes seek out any form of comfort they could find. Even if that comfort came at the cost of being a voluntary victim.

But that scenario didn't quite add up either—thanks largely to the fact that the media had only given the theft a small blip of coverage. It had made national news, that was true. But it had been quickly upstaged by a public school shooting and yet another gun control debate that led to yet another round of teeth gnashing and ineffective bickering. Abbey Cooper and her stolen arm had sunken below the fold quickly, and since then Abbey hadn't done anything to rekindle the limelight, as far as Alex could determine.

Which didn't necessarily eliminate Abbey as a suspect, of course.

But from what Alex had observed—and she was willing to admit that this was pure gut instinct—but Abbey just didn't read as the type to do this. It was possible, sure. But unlikely. Alex's intuition was telling her it just wasn't the right track.

Still, she'd make sure to eliminate that as a possibility, if she could. Better to spend the time and be double sure. If it did turn out that Abbey was the one...

Well, Alex would just move on. No more contact. No retaliation. If Abbey stole the arm herself, it was for some sad and, honestly, understandable reasons. Alex would let her go about the rest of her life.

Her final pass before leaving Abbey's place was to get shots of the outside of the apartments.

She had saved this for last, just in case any of Eric's people were around and she'd have to make a run for it. The fastest way to get the shots she needed was to capture video footage in 4K, using a GoPro camera. She had one mounted on a 3-way stick, oriented so she could hold on to it near her waist while running it along at a low angle. She repeated the move with the camera at a high angle, capturing everything from the top down. She'd use this, along with footage of the roof she'd snagged from across the street earlier, to reconstruct the building from the outside. That, along with the photos and footage of the apartment, and should have a pretty good virtual landscape to explore.

She slipped away when the footage was done and made her way to an apartment complex miles away. Using QuIEK she was able to open the door to the business center of the complex, a room with comfortable chairs and rows of iMac computers, plus a conference room with a door she could close and lock. The apartments had a first-come-first-served policy for these amenities, unless they'd been booked in advance. Alex had booked them on behalf of a tenant who wasn't at all likely to come anywhere near the space.

Now in a secure and comfortable place, with a Keurig and coffee pods close at hand, she got to work.

All the footage had been uploaded to Smokescreen, where it was being processed and stitched together by thousands of microprocessors spread over North America. QuIEK made it possible for them to work at high speeds—faster than would have been possible with the lag that came from mismatched

WiFi. Alex had set up Smokescreen to co-opt priority when she needed more processing power.

It was like having the world's fastest server in the room with her, taking up only the space of her laptop.

Alex brought up everything on the small laptop she'd procured that morning, and once the 3D processing was done, she could move around in the virtual space, as if she were standing in it. She could even zoom in for more detail, thanks to the high-resolution scans.

Next time, she thought, *I get the LiDAR.*

Light Detection and Ranging, or *LiDAR*, was an emerging technology that had all sorts of applications for scanning a space and recreating it in 3D. It could even unpeel layers of the scene to help reveal hidden secrets. LiDAR was being used by surveyors to find deposits of minerals and other resources, and by archaeologists to find lost cities in overgrown jungles. Recently, it had become a more consumer-oriented product, starting to turn up in iPads and other tech.

She hadn't gotten around to using it yet, but it would have certainly come in handy here, she figured.

Next time.

Alex scanned her way through the apartment again, running through it almost in the same pattern she'd used while visiting the real space. She then virtually walked around and even flew over the building from the outside, looking for anything that might spark some ideas. There had to be something, in this virtual map of the place, that could give her a lead. *Any* lead.

She paused.

On the screen she was looking at a corner of the building's exterior where a series of half-assed repairs had been made. The building was sheathed in an off-white stucco, and in one corner, at approximately where Abbey and Rachel's ceiling would be, there was a terrible looking patch of plywood and paint. The sort of thing a cheap landlord would do, rather than pay a professional to fix it.

Alex pushed in on the patch, expanding it on screen and bringing some of its detail into focus. The closer she got, the less resolution she'd have. But at 4K she could get in close enough to get a decent look.

The patch showed some sign of weathering, which probably meant it had been there for at least a year. It was impossible to know if it had been done prior to or after the theft, but Alex was putting her money on after.

She wasn't sure how this could relate to Abbey's arm, but that gut instinct was nagging at her again.

Weren't there photos of the exterior from the initial investigation?

Alex pulled up the folder from the FBI's servers and sifted through the images, stopping when she came to the exterior of the building.

There were only three photos, unfortunately, and they were largely focused on the various ground-floor exits. One photo, however, was a wider shot of the building itself. When she looked closely, zooming in to the point just before the pixels made the shape unreadable, she could just make out a dark spot in the same location as the patch.

It looked like a gaping hole in the building's exterior.

Alex thought about this and struggled to make sense of it.

Somehow, at a height much greater than what someone could reach without a ladder, a chunk of the building's exterior was damaged and missing. And it just happened to align with Abbey's apartment.

Alex might have no way of knowing if the damage had existed prior to the theft, but in an *Occam's Razor* sort of way, it seemed unlikely.

Strings of coincidence usually knotted around the most significant known facts. The simplest answers were usually the right answers.

She went back to the virtual walk-thru of the apartment.

To her disappointment, there was nothing to see in the corner near where the damage would be outside. In fact, that section of the ceiling was blocked by a hanging air duct that ran along the ceiling, covered in sheetrock to make a soffit. No damage to the soffit or the walls. Nothing that corresponded to the damage outside the building.

Alex considered this, then rotated the view of the apartment, stopping when she saw what she was looking for. She zoomed in and leaned forward.

Filling the screen nearly from edge to edge was a rectangular vent that led into the ductwork. It was affixed to the soffit wall by a single screw at the top. At the bottom was an empty threaded hole where a second screw should be.

It was a pretty tiny lead—literally only the size of a screw hole. But something about it tickled the back of her brain. It was just too much of a coincidence. It *had* to connect, somehow.

But what could it possibly mean?

The vent was maybe twelve by six inches at most. The hole it covered would be a bit smaller than that. The duct work couldn't have been much larger.

Certainly there was no way anyone could wriggle through either, to sneak into the apartment or make their escape. They'd have to be a foot tall, at most. Or really, really thin. Short of highly trained babies or reanimated skeletons, Alex was drawing a blank on how anyone might get in and out of there.

Still... it was the first evidence of a way in and out that didn't involve unlocking and re-locking the front door. It was impossible. But it was the only way.

So what did it mean?

She scanned the rest of the images, picking at them bit by bit and pixel by pixel, trying to spot anything else that might be connected. She overlaid the images from the initial investigation, integrating them as part of the 3D model she'd constructed, and still found nothing useful.

Another dead end?

This case was full of them. They were stacking up like cordwood, and it was starting to feel dangerous. The heat was on, with the FBI so close. Even with the games Alex was playing with them, she wouldn't be able to evade them forever. Not if she stayed in one place.

She needed a break in this. She needed for something to click.

She cursed and shook her head, suddenly realizing exactly what she had to do next.

She needed to ask for help.

CHAPTER SEVENTEEN

SYMON WALKED into the lobby of the Disney Boardwalk hotel. It was the fifth resort he'd visited that day, and if he was being honest this entire line of investigation was starting to wear on him. If he never saw a pair of mouse ears again, it would be too soon.

He had his people scouring the parks, watching the monorail and the buses, monitoring Disney's extensive (and he had to admit, ridiculously impressive) security footage. They'd found hints of her, looking back at footage from the past week. Alex Kayne in her various guises, spotted by agents trained in facial recognition. She'd been here. His hunch had been right.

He approached the concierge and showed his badge. "I need to see reservations for everyone who has checked in over the past couple of weeks."

The concierge, an older man who was flustered by the very un-Disney request, nodded and complied. "I can show you all of the guest information, but there's quite a bit."

"How many people have checked in?" Symon asked.

The concierge looked at him. "Hundreds," he said. "In two

weeks we could have thousands of guests check in and check out."

Symon nodded. He'd heard this before, of course. Which made it no less daunting. He'd personally checked registries with four other resorts and had handed off results to the tech team to analyze. They'd look for patterns and try to narrow things down.

It was going to take time. Maybe too much time.

He always made the first pass, though. He wasn't even sure what he was looking for, but he had the distinct feeling he'd know it when he saw it. There was sure to be something. Some telltale sign, some detail that would pop out at him.

The concierge brought up all the recent reservations and then stepped aside, holding out his palm to invite Symon to take the reins.

He stepped forward and started scanning through the list.

Immediately he skipped back by four days. It was always possible Alex had checked in during that time, and if she did, he would trust the tech team to find her. His instincts were telling him that she'd checked in much earlier, though. She'd gone on the run after they'd found her Airbnb, and he didn't think she'd had a reservation here as part of her backup plan. He couldn't know for sure, of course. Again, it was instinct. But he thought she'd had to improvise a little.

Running through the reservations, he paused at one that caught his eye.

It was for a family of four—mom, dad, and two kids, a girl and a boy. Not an unusual reservation, by any stretch. There were hundreds of others just like it.

But the name...

Erin and Julie Simon.

That couldn't be a coincidence.

It wasn't exactly his surname, of course. His was a variant

spelling, and this was more traditional. But the fact that it was *Erin* and *Julie*—a slight skewing on Eric Symon and Julia Mayher—that was just too much. It felt like the kind of thing Alex Kayne would do, taking their names and using them to hide in plain site.

"This one," he said, pointing. "I need the key to their room."

The concierge nodded and created a keycard for him.

Symon used the backup phone and called Agent Mayher. "Bring them in," he said. "I think we have her."

AGENTS SURROUNDED the room from both sides, and Symon made sure two more agents were also stationed on the ground outside, watching the window. Kayne had proven that height and gravity were no barriers.

He made a gesture, signaling Mayher and the others, and then he swiped the door key. There was a beep and a click, and they rushed into the room in a cacophony of orders to show hands and to get down.

The room was mostly empty.

Alex was nowhere to be seen, which was not altogether unexpected. Symon figured that even if this was her room, she was likely out doing the things she did, whatever those things might be.

But there were signs that the room was hers.

Annoying signs.

Laid out on the bed were a couple of changes of clothes as well as a couple of wigs, some hats, and multiple pairs of sunglasses. All of this was arranged in much the way someone would pick out clothes for various activities thought a day at Disney. Outfits for the park, for dinner, for a night out with or maybe without the kids. Only the wigs seemed out of place.

On the little desk near the window there was a smart tablet. And stuck to this was a pink Post-It note that had *Eric* written on it.

He looked at Mayher, who shrugged. "Not surprising that she made us," she said.

He nodded. Not surprising. Just frustrating, as usual. He didn't look forward to the chewing out that would inevitably come.

He picked up the tablet. It wasn't secured, and he was able to open it without a PIN code. He discovered that a video player was already loaded.

He pushed play.

Alex Kayne appeared on screen.

"Well hey there, Eric!" she said, waving. She was wearing a pair of Minnie Mouse ears and a Walt Disney T-shirt. Mayher quickly pulled up her phone and showed Symon a still that agents had taken from a camera in Epcot. It showed Alex Kayne, dressed exactly as she was in the video, standing out in the open as if she wanted the cameras to see her.

Which, Symon knew, she had.

The still image was dated two days earlier. Meaning Alex had likely moved on days ago, leaving all of this behind as a tantalizing distraction for Symon and his team to chase down, while she stayed safely out of reach. Again.

"I know... big *bummer* that I'm not there. Especially after you cracked my super-secret code in the reservations. I know that's annoying. But listen, I have a favor to ask."

"You've more or less figured out my shtick. But let me just give you the full breakdown of how things work. Call this a peace offering. I'm giving you valuable intel on your fugitive."

"You made the connection between Uconic and Shortel, I

know. That connection is Abbey Cooper. She's an amputee who had her high-tech experimental prosthetic stolen. Consider this official confirmation of your theory. You're on the right track."

"The thing is, I'm here to find out who took it, and to return it if I can. And the *problem* is, I've run into a dead end. A few of them, actually. Part of that is because I have you guys hawking my every move. Congrats and keeping me preoccupied. But the downside to you guys being so close to nabbing *me* is that Abbey may not get her arm back, and some bad guys may get away. And that... well look, Eric, I'm going to be straight with you. That's something I can't allow."

"So I have a proposition. I'd like you to help me track this down and bring some justice for Abbey. It's already an FBI case, so you won't even be stepping on anyone's toes."

"Right now, since you opened this video, there's a bunch of data downloading to that special phone I told you to hang onto. I'm giving you everything I've uncovered so far, including stuff I pulled from the FBI's own database. This is it. This is everything I have on this case."

"The thing is, giving you this stuff opens me up to some vulnerability. So I'm just going to play that card for all it's worth. I'm going to give you something. Call it a token of good faith."

"Here's the deal: When I take on one of these jobs, I have to see it all the way to the end. I don't leave until the job is finished. It doesn't matter how many close calls I have with you guys, how often I have to find a way to escape. I won't run. Ever. Not until I've solved this for Abbey, or for any other client. So that's my kryptonite, Eric. That's my weakness."

"This is my purpose. It's what keeps me from losing it, while I'm out here, on the run from you and the NSA and everyone else. I find someone who needs my help, and I help them. And that keeps me sane. It gives me a reason to keep going. You can call that delusion, if it makes you feel better. Just me trying to fool me, and maybe you, into believing I'm a good person after all, yada yada. I know what my profile says. So... don't believe me when I say I'm innocent. But delusion or not, this is who I am and what I do. It's my vulnerability."

"Now that you know this, you can use it to help hunt me down. It's valuable information, actually. You now know that if you find a trace of me somewhere, it means someone needs my help. And if that someone's trouble hasn't been resolved, it means I'm still there. I'm not leaving. I stay until the job is done."

"That could be the thing you use to bring me in. So... you're welcome. My gift to you. But I'm more than willing to throw you that bone if you'll please help to find Abbey Cooper's arm. Help me solve that, and you might actually catch me. I'm going to be working this case myself, so you could even catch me before it's all done. If so, all I ask is that you keep at this. Find Abbey's arm. Find who took it. Get it back to her."

"That's it. I hope you and the other agents at least enjoyed some time at Disney World. I'm long gone, of course, but how could I resist a couple of days at the happiest place on earth?"

She paused, smiled, took in a deep breath and let it out with a rush.

"See you soon, Eric."

The video went black, and it didn't take long to realize that the tablet had been wiped completely clean. No chance of recovery. Everything on it would smell like bleach at this point.

Symon raised his eyebrows and exchanged a look with Mayher.

"Damn. Is it ok that I like her, just a little?" Mayher asked.

Symon shook his head. "Dammit."

"So what are we going to do now?" Mayher asked.

"The same thing we've been doing all along," Symon replied. "We're going to find Alex Kayne. But..."

Mayher gave him a wry look. "But?"

"If we can find Abbey Cooper's arm, we'll do that too." He looked at Mayher and rolled his eyes. "Kayne is the priority. But we can't ignore a lead in an ongoing case. We'll take a look at what she sent us, too."

He thought for a moment, shook his head, cursed again. "And I think it's time we talk to Abbey Cooper."

CHAPTER EIGHTEEN

THE MARITEF OFFICES looked more like a travel agent's domain than a research center.

Symon understood that this was part of the strategy. Maritef's ecotourism business increased interest in their ecological research and recovery work, by promoting the oceans as a beautiful tourist location. Getting the public excited about the wonders of marine life was the first punch, and the second was showing them how all of it was in jeopardy unless someone was willing to help. Donations and volunteers tended to go up after rounds of tours. It was a good business model.

Abbey Cooper was wearing a blue Maritef vest over her street clothes. Her left sleeve was folded and clasped with a stylish looking pin.

Symon was pleasantly surprised to see that she didn't favor the lost arm at all. She moved and behaved as if nothing were wrong, showing no signs of self-consciousness. It showed some of her character. It made him root for her.

In the video interviews taken after the theft she had seemed somehow smaller, more timid and defeated. It could be that in the intervening year since the theft, Abbey had come to grips with some things.

But Symon thought it might be the job. Here, at Maritef, she was just one of the researchers. She had a challenge to work around, but it didn't keep her from being a part of the team, or from doing the work she was passionate about. The loss of her arm hadn't truncated her goals, even if it might have changed how she got to them.

She might be a completely different person, when she wasn't on the job. But here she was in her element, and her confidence was evident, even though she seemed a bit hesitant about talking to the FBI.

"Have you made some progress?" she asked, a glint of hope in her eyes.

Symon shook his head, though he was smiling lightly. "No, I'm sorry, we're really only just getting back to this, to be honest. There have been no new breaks in the case since the initial investigation." He hesitated a moment, then said, "Except for the person currently looking into the case."

He watched her face, and though it took a moment, he saw her expression as she realized who he meant. The smile faded somewhat from her lips.

"It's ok," he said. "We know about her."

"I don't really know who she is. She hasn't been in touch since we met. She told me not to talk about what she was doing, but she must be working with you?"

Symon smiled and nodded. "Something like that," he said. It wouldn't do any good to tell Abbey the full story, and there were details he couldn't reveal at any rate. He also didn't want to cause her any more grief. It wasn't her fault that she'd been contacted by a fugitive. Abbey was just hoping someone, *anyone*, would help her. The people she'd initially turned to for help had more or less put her file on the back burner.

Alex Kayne must have felt like a ray of hope for a case that had been seemingly forgotten.

That galled Symon.

He knew that it was part of the job, that not every case could be solved or could even warrant the sort of resources needed to make headway. Every case was important. Every case had eyes on it and minds working it. But in the rush of things, with new acts of terror and kidnappings and harmful things done to children—not to mention tracking fugitives on the run—it was easy for something like this to get set aside.

Even with the implications of classified technology associated with this case, there would be a tendency for agents to have to move on to something else, in the absence of any leads.

Meanwhile there was the human cost.

Abbey Cooper, who had already suffered a horrific tragedy, had once again lost something that impacted her life in myriad ways. She had adapted, because that was who she was. She was strong and capable, Symon could see that. But that didn't make the crime any more acceptable. The fact that it had gone cold seemed like compounded injustice.

"Ms. Cooper, has there been anything over the past year that might bring new light to the case? Has anyone ever contacted you?"

She shook her head. "Until this lady reached out to me, I really thought I'd never hear anything about it again. Uconic's CEO wrote me a letter a couple of months after the investigation had sort of played out, explaining why they wouldn't be able to replace the arm."

"What did he say?" Symon asked.

She thought for a moment. "It was all about their contracts and non-disclosure agreements. Some of the terms had changed in a few government contracts, he said. I... well, I kind of got mad about it all."

Symon nodded. "I bet. Do you still have the letter?"

"I think it's at home. I was keeping a file for a while. I don't know why. I guess I thought I might play justice warrior or something. But Uconic had been so nice to me before this, and I figured it wasn't really their fault if things had changed. I can look for that letter tonight."

"I'd appreciate that," Symon nodded. He looked around the room, hesitating before going on. "About the woman—how did she reach out to you, initially?"

"I got a text message," Abbey said. "It was an update on my case, telling me that even though there was no new evidence, someone was still looking into it."

"Did she identify herself in the text?" Symon asked.

"She said she was a free agent, and that she was picking up the case file from the FBI."

All true, Symon thought, *as far as it goes*.

"Do you still have that text?"

She took out her phone and placed it on the table in front of her, swiping through it. "Here it is," she said, handing it to him.

He looked through the exchange. The number was from DC, but Alex could have easily spoofed that. "Do you mind if I forward this to myself?" Symon asked.

She shook her head, and he then sent the message and a screenshot to his alternate phone and to Agent Mayher's phone.

I'll explain later, he wrote.

He handed the phone back to Abbey. "So that's it? No other messages or contacts about this? Nothing unusual at home?"

She hesitated. "Well... ok, I didn't really think this could have anything to do with anything. But after my arm was stolen, about a month later, I got a weird cell phone bill."

"Weird how?" Symon asked.

"I didn't have unlimited data then," she said. "And there were some overages on my data plan. I had maybe 20 gigabytes of data at the time, and I somehow burned through that and did another forty that month. I use my phone for practically everything, but I'd never used that much data at once."

"And you think that has something to do with your arm?"

She laughed, self conscious. "It's just kind of a feeling, you know? I don't really think it has anything to do with it, now, but at the time I was kind of freaked out, and everything seemed like it might be connected. I wanted to change the locks on the apartment, but the building manager wouldn't let me do it, and he never got around to doing it himself. I was kind of a mess, and everything that happened seemed like it might be someone trying to get to me."

Symon had taken out the small notepad he kept in his pocket and made a note. "Can you send me a copy of the bill?" he asked.

"Yes," she said, and immediately started tapping her phone. A moment later he was pinged with a new text message and saw a digital version of the bill. "They refunded half of the cost. I guess that was nice, they were really kind of jerks about the whole thing. They didn't believe me. But a few weeks later I upgraded to unlimited. I haven't noticed a spike like that since."

Symon was studying the bill, which wasn't entirely helpful. It didn't break down how the data was used, or when. Details that even the consumer should have a right to see, he thought.

"I have a favor to ask," he said to Abbey. "Can you contact your mobile carrier and ask them to provide me detailed records of this? If I request this myself, I have to go through channels, get warrants, and basically burn a lot of time. This is one instance where the consumer has a little more power than I do."

"Ok," she nodded. "I can call them now, if you like."

He nodded, and as she called and started talking to her provider he left the room, returning to the break room where he'd been shown a fridge full of beverages. He took out two bottles of water, figuring to bring one to Abbey. Instead of heading straight back to the conference room, he leaned against the kitchen counter and mentally sifted through what he'd gathered so far.

There was a ping from his pocket.

He took out the phone that Alex Kayne had told him to keep on him, and saw that the message was from her.

I just looked into those phone records, she'd written. *All of that data was used in one burst. Around 90GB. That's way more than your average Netflix binge, and it happened in about an hour on the same day Abbey's arm was taken.*

Symon's eyebrows went up. He'd worry about how Alex had tracked his conversation with Abbey later. For now, he was more curious about the data burst.

What would cause a burst like that? he asked.

There was a pause while three little animated dots pulsed at the bottom of the screen, before a new text appeared.

It could be a number of things, but I don't think it's a coincidence at all. The mobile company is giving Abbey the runaround, but I just emailed you everything they have on her data usage from that period. The IP her phone connected to was run through a VPN that bounced it all over the planet. I might be able to back trace that, but it could take weeks. Let me work on this.

Symon shook his head and smiled.

So it's kind of like looking for you, he responded. *Maybe it's karma.*

The dots were back briefly, then a smiley face emoji appeared, along with the words *Maybe.*

Symon slipped the *Alex Phone*—as he'd started calling it—back into his pocket and took out his alternate phone. He checked his email and found the file that Alex had promised. He spent a moment scanning it, but it may as well have been Greek for all he could make of it. He forwarded it to the tech team, with a CC to Mayher. He wanted to keep her in the loop as much as possible.

In case I'm fired over this, he thought.

There was a reason he'd chosen to interview Abbey Cooper alone. He wanted to insulate Mayher and the rest of his team from this. To anyone outside, it could appear that he was colluding with Alex Kayne. Given his history, and the implications that had hung over his connection to Director Crispen, something like this could be a career ender.

If so, his was the only career he was willing to risk.

He was back on unsteady ground again, and no more comfortable for its familiarity. It seemed like he'd only just gotten back into the good graces of his superiors, convincing them that he was willing to play ball, though he'd never done anything wrong in the first place.

Now, though, here he was, outside the field and not even wearing his catcher's mitt. It would be easy enough for someone to assume that he was playing ball, alright—just for the other team.

There was sure to be a stern word or two coming his way, at the very least, considering his task was to apprehend Alex Kayne, not work with her. He'd already written a report and had it ready to go, outlining his plan to keep Kayne engaged so they could find a way to track her down. It was well written and thought out and sounded like BS to him as much as it would to the Director. But it did have some merit to recommend it.

For the first time in two years, they were in frequent

contact with Alex Kayne. No one, in all that time, had talked to her at all.

Agent Symon had her on speed dial.

That would help things, he figured. The FBI did understand the concept of nurturing a relationship with a suspect, luring them into complacency. He figured he could leverage that for some goodwill. The more contact he had with the fugitive, the more they would learn about her, and the greater the chance they'd find a way to bring her in.

And if they helped Abbey Cooper and closed a cold case in the process, that was good too.

By the time Symon sifted through everything in his head and carried the bottles of water back to the conference room, he'd almost convinced himself that wasn't going to see a lot of trouble over this.

Almost.

CHAPTER NINETEEN

THE DATA SURGE was something she should have caught.

Alex had looked at Abbey's phone records for the 90-day period leading up to the theft, and she'd looked through her browsing and search history on both her phone and her laptop. She'd found nothing that she thought might have been related at the time. But she'd never even considered looking at the amount of data used on her phone.

That was significant. And she had missed it.

Now that she had Abbey's usage records for the months prior and following the theft, she could see at a glance that the surge wasn't part of a pattern. It indicated something. *What*, exactly, was still up for grabs. But Alex could already sense some of the holes filling in.

The VPN was traceable, with enough time, but time was something Alex simply didn't have. She had managed to cajole Agent Symon into helping to solve this, and she had to admit— she wouldn't have found this lead without him. His interview instincts were on point, and the fact that he could freely chat with Abbey, without looking over his shoulder, had to have been a benefit. Plus, he had good instincts, following up on exactly what Alex would have herself.

He made for a good ally.

But she couldn't forget that he and the rest of his team were still actively looking to bring her in. Goodwill or not, common interests or not, eventually Agent Eric Symon would find her. The clock was ticking.

Something to deal with at another time, Alex thought.

For the moment, she had to deal with a new frustration.

Though she could *see* the surge in Abbey's data usage, she couldn't see the data itself. She couldn't even determine whether it was incoming or outgoing, thanks to the vague records kept by the mobile carrier. The best she could manage was to determine that the surge was 90 gigabytes of data in about an hour. A lot, in other words. Something big was moved over the network, in a relatively short amount of time.

Definitely not Netflix.

Alex was sitting on a deck overlooking the water, shaded by the flowing linen curtains of a rented cabana. She wasn't far from Eric's current location, really. If he'd known where to find her, he could have her surrounded in under twenty minutes. Maybe ten.

To ensure she was safe enough, however, she had booked rooms in dozens of hotels all around Orlando, using a variety of names that would immediately be recognized by Symon and his people. She then swizzled those reservations, so that they pointed to actual rooms with actual guests.

A lot of people were getting free stays this week, courtesy of QuIEK.

It had taken hours to set it all up, but the ruse would be enough of a smokescreen (no pun intended) to let her have some breathing room for a few days. There was virtually no danger of being recognized here, at her current location, either.

Because for now, at least, Alex had no intention of leaving this private cabana, which directly butted up against her very expensive, private suite, in an exclusive resort that cost more per night than most people paid in rent each month.

QuIEK Card—membership had its privileges.

She didn't like doing this sort of thing often. For one, it was ostentatious, and could backfire by earning her a level of scrutiny and attention she didn't want—wait staff and resort management liked to get to know their guests, to better see to their needs. Alex eschewed this attention as much as possible, but people trained to remember little details were often resourceful in finding out everything they could.

And of course, there were the ethical concerns. QuIEK gave her an infinite bank account, but the money still came from *somewhere*. And though she was always careful to siphon money from businesses and individuals who were typically "not-so-nice," it was still stealing, after all. Alex stole as a means of survival, but she was aware of the great karmic debt she incurred.

She wasn't altogether superstitious, but she definitely believed there was a balance to the universe. Whatever good karma she earned by being innocent of the charges against her, and by the work she did for others, it was likely balanced out thanks to the means by which she survived. Not a justification, in her view. Just the facts of her existence.

So when she splurged, as she was doing now, the weight of it really hit home. Anxiety, guilt, and a constant ethical itch plagued her.

Mostly.

Mojitos and in-suite massages could occasionally push all of that to the background.

No mojitos or massages at the moment, however. She was working.

Alex leaned back, stretching, and reached for the iced tea that was gathering condensation in the Orlando humidity. She sipped, and she thought.

What's 90 GB and takes an hour to download or upload?

It was a sphinx-worthy riddle if she'd ever heard one, and it was making her head hurt, running through it in a loop.

Worse, there was the bonus riddle:

What does 90 GB data surge have to do with a stolen prosthetic arm?

She was starting to grow frustrated with the problem, which triggered Papa Kayne's voice in her head.

When you're not getting answers, ask different questions.

It was one of his favorites, but it had always driven Alex nuts. If she came to him with a problem, she was always hopeful for a solution. Which was ridiculous, because he invariably made her figure it out for herself.

You're asking one question, but you're looking for the answer to another, he'd say. *When you're not getting answers, ask different questions.*

Different questions.

Right now, she was asking the same questions on repeat: What sort of data surge would total up to 90GB? What could Abbey have downloaded or uploaded that would account for that kind of surge? Did that relate to the theft? Or was it coincidence?

She was getting nowhere in that loop.

But what if she was focused on the wrong user?

Abbey had already said she hadn't even known about the surge. She didn't do anything, in her personal life or career, that would require that much data in one burst.

But what would the *arm* do with 90 GB?

Alex returned her attention to her laptop and moments later QuIEK opened up the way for her to once again peek into the plans and specs for the UPP8. This time, however, she turned her attention away from the hardware and focused entirely on the software.

The operating system was built on a proprietary platform, but it shared characteristics with a few open-source Linux-based systems. Enough so that Alex didn't even need QuIEK to sift through the source code. She was familiar with these, having used them in early approaches for developing QuIEK.

The problem was, nothing in the arm's operating system came anywhere near 90 GB. At most, the whole thing topped out at 60GB, which nearly maxed out its internal storage. The AI running and articulating the arm wasn't load-heavy. The arm's entire operating system was stored on a tiny, lightweight memory card.

Different questions, then, Alex thought.

It all came back to assumptions.

What if this stream of data wasn't simply a download or upload?

What if it was *both?*

She'd been working from the assumption that the 90 GB surge had been one-way, but what if it wasn't? What if that was a cumulative number, totaling data uploading and downloading over that one-hour timeframe?

She looked closer at the arm's OS. The core system, The managing AI, was maybe 5 GB. Very streamlined. Alex was impressed.

The other 55 GB was mostly code used to manage and control the various sensors and actuators of the arm. Code that made the arm rise when Abbey willed it to rise, to squeeze when she willed it to squeeze.

The sensory code was there to translate information gathered from an array of sensors into impulses that would be fed into Abbey's surgically implanted interface, where additional processing would take place. It was a multi-part, symbiotic system that worked in a way that Alex could only describe as *poetic*.

She was very impressed.

And only became more so as she kept digging.

The arm had a wireless interface, so that it could be programmed and updated. The system used Bluetooth, so that Uconic's lab techs could use handheld devices to program and update the arm without Abbey having to remove it, or without the need to connect cables to it.

Bluetooth.

Alex laughed and could have smacked herself.

Someone had hacked Abbey's phone, had then connected to the arm via Bluetooth, and had then downloaded and uploaded data to its operating system. Data that contained new instructions and new protocols.

Data that totaled 90 GB.

It fit. It was neat. But it still left questions.

So someone hacked the arm. What did that amount to? How did that lead to the theft? How did a data transfer end with the arm disappearing from Abbey's apartment, with apparently no one entering or exiting?

Alex could only think of one way. And it was...

Well, it was *ridiculous*.

It was absurd to the point of making her groan to even consider it. But there it was. From an infinite array of impossible scenarios, it all narrowed down to just one possibility. Like the observer effect in quantum physics—now that she could *see it*, the answer became obvious. Even if it was unlikely.

Or, to put it in Sherlockian terms: She could finally eliminate all the impossible, and that left only this single, improbable truth.

The arm had stolen itself.

She groaned and pinched the bridge of her nose.

It made sense. Sort of. It added up. Kind of. It was the only answer that fit the evidence, which she couldn't refute. Still...

It was ridiculous.

For now.

"Ok, so I'm getting nowhere," she said aloud.

Short of someone hacking the arm to make it autonomous, and then having the arm crawl its way out of Abbey Cooper's bedroom, Alex still didn't have any real answers to this.

Except...

Sure, it was ridiculous that the arm would steal itself. But that data stream *meant something*. Alex couldn't know what modifications were made to the arm's operating system without examining it, however.

Or could she?

There were two prototypes of the UPP prosthetic being developed at Uconic.

She looked now at the operating system for the UPPX, comparing it side-by-side with the 8.

They were pretty similar, but not exactly the same. In fact there were a number of key differences between the two, including some potent code changes laced throughout the operating system.

She kept sifting through it and referenced the UPPX's documentation.

"Not so ridiculous..." she said, shaking her head in disbelief.

The X prototype was a military-grade piece of technology. The program surrounding its development had several aims, but one of those was a protocol for protecting the secrets of the tech. If the arm were to be used in combat, there had to be safeguards in place, to ensure that the technology couldn't fall into enemy hands.

Some of the code in the X's operating system was meant to create a full scale meltdown, a cascading failure in all of the arm's sensors and actuators. Basically it had the ability to reroute its own power supply and fry everything.

A self-destruct protocol.

But there was a *secondary* protocol. One that was a little macabre, but still pretty cool.

If a soldier went down in combat, injured or killed, the arm could attempt a *self extraction*.

It could activate its own actuators and sensors and use them to detach from its host and literally *claw* its way to a safe hiding place. From there it could start transmitting a rescue beacon.

Eventually the good guys would find it, access any intel it had gathered, and use that against the enemy.

Oh, and rescue the fallen soldier, of course. Which Alex thought was awfully nice of them, considering they were ghouls.

It was ridiculous, and the implications of it all were still tough to discern. But it fit.

Someone had used Abbey Cooper's phone to hack her prosthetic arm and to replace its operating system with that of the UPPX. There were some sensors and circuitry missing from the UUP8, but from what Alex could determine there was no reason the hacker couldn't get this close enough to work.

It was absurd. But it was plausible. In fact, it was the only explanation that fit.

So why?

And who?

Alex had been holding on to the hope that if she figured out the *how*, the *who* and the *why* would click into place. But if anything, she now felt she was further away from those answers than ever.

Back to motives.

What was the benefit of stealing the UPP8?

She sipped her iced tea.

Question: What do you get when you cross Abbey Cooper's UPP8 arm with the UPPX operating system?

Answer: A head start.

Unlike the UPPX prototypes, the UPP8 was accessible. It was vulnerable.

Functionally it was nearly identical to its upgraded big brother, with just a few bits and pieces making the difference. The bulk of the tech was there, and if someone had access to the UPPX operating system, then they likely had access to the specs. They could potentially fill in the gaps.

Ok, Alex thought. *Ok, it's a start. We have a* how, *and we have a* why.

That only left *who.*

Who had access to the code and the specs? Who would need to steal the arm to get the final piece?

There were no obvious answers. There weren't even any hints. Everyone who had access to all of that would have no need to steal Abbey's arm. They already had everything they'd need...

Unless...

What other assumption was Alex clinging to? What was she taking as a given?

Her *Alex-sense* was tingling again, but this time her intuition was pointing her to something Abbey had said to Agent Symon. Something Abbey was going to find for him when she was off work.

Alex picked up the laptop and slipped back into her room. It looked like she wasn't going to lay low after all.

She was about to do something stupid.

But if she was right, it might finally crack this.

She just had to get to it before Eric Symon did.

CHAPTER TWENTY

SYMON and Mayher were perusing Abbey Cooper's file over drinks. Officially they were off duty, but in Symon's experience "off duty" was never really a thing in the FBI. The work tended to intrude on every moment, in one way or another.

"Off duty" was really just a way of saying it was ok to have a drink while you worked.

"Do we have a copy of the government contracts?" Mayher asked.

"On their way," Symon replied, shuffling through the rest of the letters and papers Abbey had gathered for them.

There wasn't much, and it didn't add enough to the story to really make an opening. But it did raise more questions—as if they hadn't had enough of those.

Mayher leaned back and held her glass of scotch near her chest. "We're sure this will lead us to Alex Kayne?" she asked.

Symon looked up, sighed, and picked up his own drink.

"It's the best lead we have at the moment. We know that she's out to solve this for Abbey. That lets us have some insight into what's driving her, which may help us track her."

"Has it so far?" Mayher asked, sipping her scotch.

Symon shook his head. "Not particularly. But it's only been a few days. Give it time."

"Do we have that time? Because as far as I can tell, the second Abbey's case is resolved Kayne is in the wind again, and this time she's leaving town."

That point had not escaped Symon's attention. He knew that Alex was watching them. He knew that she had access to any evidence the FBI found. And he knew that she'd run, once Abbey had justice. He was hoping he might be able to solve this and keep it from Alex long enough to leverage it, to make her show herself. But the odds were stacked against that.

"There's Abbey Cooper to consider in this, too," he said. "She's a victim. The case is on the FBI's docket, so if we can solve it we're still doing our jobs."

"But we aren't fulfilling our mission," Mayher said.

Symon nodded. "Which is why I have other agents continuing to work the case from the outside."

Mayher thought about this. "A distraction?"

Symon said nothing but sipped his drink.

"We're a *distraction*?" Mayher repeated. She laughed. "I should have seen that."

"Don't be too hard on yourself. It isn't what I wanted. I'd like to be there when we take her in. But Kayne has made me. She's somehow tapped into my phone and was able to track everything we discussed in that conference room."

"So what's preventing her from overhearing us right now?"

Symon gestured around the bar. "No cameras. I left both of my phones in my room."

"I have mine," Mayher said, then blinked. "But you asked me to turn it off." She gave a quick shake of her head, and made a strange expression, as if suddenly realizing something. "I thought..."

"What?" Symon asked.

There was a slight blush to Mayher's cheek, but she shook her head. "I thought that was a little weird. Ok, so we're in a pocket of privacy right now. Want to share anything with me that we wouldn't want Kayne to overhear?"

"You have all of it. We're working Abbey Cooper's case as a way to keep Alex Kayne looking the wrong direction. The rest of my team is keeping the heat on, with orders to report to me only when I've arranged it."

"Ok then," Mayher nodded. She looked from him to the papers in front of them. "So in the meantime, let's solve this. In for one impossible case, in for a dozen."

"Just the two," Symon smiled. He leaned forward and tapped the letter from Roderick Verice. "A heartfelt apology to a girl who was a huge PR boost for Uconic."

"He couldn't help it if the terms of the contract changed."

"So the government clamped down on the tech. The military is getting not just first dibs, but *all* dibs. That could open a path to a motive."

"You think someone stole Abbey's prosthetic as a result of the military taking over the whole UPP project?"

Symon nodded. "Abbey's arm was a prototype. It was grandfathered into Uconic's original deal. But with the changes in the contract, Verice wasn't allowed to replace it."

"So would Verice or someone working for him have any reason to steal the arm?" Mayher asked.

Symon considered this and shook his head. "I don't think so. They have the UPPX prototype, all the designs, everything they'd need to build more. It doesn't make sense."

"So who else would be impacted by this change to the contract?"

Symon was thinking, sipping from his drink and occasionally glancing at the television above the bar. A baseball game was playing, and the pitcher had just beaned the batter with a wild pitch. The batter was shaking it off, and took off his helmet as he jogged to first base. The opposing team's coach went to the mound and was chatting with the pitcher.

"What was the name of that other business? The robotics place that Kayne broke into?"

Mayher took a deep breath and released it slowly, then said, "Shorelite Robotics."

"*They'd* be impacted by this change," Symon said, his eyes still on the game. Things had resumed, and the pitcher put a strike across the plate. The guy on first led off a bit, ready to run at the first opportunity.

Mayher seemed doubtful. "You think Shorelite stole the arm? Don't they have their own version of the prototype?"

"Unless they were told they'd have to turn it over. They're a robotics company, right? They helped with the development of the UPP tech. Why?"

"They're building tech for use in everything from deep sea to space exploration. Robotics for extreme conditions," Mayher said. "The UPP program gives them some proprietary tech that puts them ahead of the competition."

"So without the UPP stuff they'd basically have to start from scratch," Symon said.

"You think they did it?"

He wasn't sure. The pieces fit. There was motive. But he'd personally interviewed Tim Davis himself, along with several of his staff. There'd been nothing to indicate that they were in any sort of trouble. They had things on track.

Symon realized, however, that he'd been working from the assumption that they still had their contract with Uconic.

What if they didn't? What if that secret, proprietary infor-mation in their safe room was under guard not because they were trying to keep contractually guarded secrets, but because they were trying to *hide something* they weren't supposed to have?

He put his glass down and checked his watch. It was after 10PM, but he could still make the call. He didn't know any local judges, but the wheels were already a little greased thanks to Alex breaking into Shorelite once already.

He could get his warrant.

If this turned out to be a bad guess, though, it was going to cost him.

"What's up?" Mayher asked.

"Turn in," he said. "Meet me in the lobby tomorrow at 6 AM."

He rose, pulling on his coat. Mayher was giving him a strange look, following his lead and getting to her feet.

"We're going back to Shorelite," Symon said.

BACK AT THE scene of the crime.

It wasn't the first time Alex had doubled back to some place she'd already explored once, but the first time she'd been here had gone just a little sideways—so she was feeling some anxiety about the whole thing.

It made her more cautious, which might be good. But it also made her jumpy, which was never a good thing.

You can't control anything in life except how you react, Papa's voice reminded her.

The close-calls, the risks, the turns that had been taken— these were all done and over. Now it was up to Alex to choose how she reacted, and to do what she needed to do.

She took a few breaths and calmed herself, then got started.

The building's security was advanced and getting this far had taken some patience and planning. Not to mention leaning heavily on her rock climbing and parkour skills. At the moment she was lowering herself out of a ceiling tile, clinging by gloved fingertips to the aluminum grid work that held the suspended ceiling in place.

It wasn't a sturdy structure—it was held up by flimsy metal strips and twisted wire. But by taking her time, moving slowly and deliberately, she was able to spider-crawl upside down until she came to the wall of a cubicle. She let her legs fall away from the ceiling while she held herself rigid by just her arms and then lowered herself until her feet met with the cubicle wall. She then dropped onto the desk, side-stepping the dual monitors and the desk phone.

She was across the room from the door she needed. She'd come in through this spot because it was in a dead zone for the motion sensors. Now, though, she'd have to wait for just a bit.

Wait and sweat.

Using Smokescreen and QuIEK, she'd gotten into the building's environmental controls and started turning things up. She kept her changes limited to this space, to keep building security from noticing anything. And while she'd made her way through the ceiling, the temperature in here had already revised upward by nearly twenty degrees.

Just a few more to go.

It was sweltering by the time Alex started to move.

The motion sensors in this room were a pretty standard PIR type—passive infrared detection that looked for a sudden rise in temperature. Gradual rises, such as what would happen if someone turned the heat up to maximum, were no problem. But if a warm body, such as a person or a pet, had moved into the relatively cooler space, the sensors would have picked it up immediately, and set off alarms.

Alex had worn thermal clothing to keep her body temperature more or less insulated from the outside, which made for a really uncomfortable infiltration, but helped to hedge against the sensors picking her up despite the high ambient temperature of the room. She was sweating, but she could move freely.

She got to the secured door and held her phone up to the security pad. There was a click, and she opened the door and stepped inside in a fluid motion.

The view was as impressive as it had been the last time she'd been to the Uconic offices.

Maybe more so in the night. From the expanse of windows she could see the castle at Magic Kingdom, lit from all angles and looking every bit as storybook as it was meant to look. As she watched, the fireworks started, illuminating the surrounding landscape in multi-colored bursts, and with booms she could hear even at this distance and even through the thick windows.

She got to work.

The last time she'd been here she'd hoped to snoop around a bit, but had been forced to improvise when Roderick Verice had bumped into her in the stairwell. The 360 scan of the place had been the best she could manage, then.

Now, as she locked the door behind her, she dove into every inch of the place, looking for anything that connected with Abbey Cooper's arm.

Verice hadn't seemed overly concerned with having her in this space, which meant either he was completely unaware of anything in here that might be compromising, or he was very confident that whatever that might be was well hidden. The assumption Alex was making, of course, was that there really was something compromising here. She was gambling, but she figured the odds were good.

She hadn't seen the letter Abbey Cooper had received, but she had seen something else—the current versions of Uconic

Prosthetic's government and military contracts. And things were worse off than Verice had implied.

The new deal made amendments to the original contract that made things a little dicey for Uconic. In essence, it had to terminate a number of outside contracts over sensitivity issues. Some classified tech was on the board to be repurposed for a variety of military uses. The US wanted a twenty-year hold on going public with the tech, while it put it to work in new programs that gave the States a prosthetic leg—or arm—up on other governments.

Uconic could continue to build its tech, but the US military would have sole access to it.

The people Roderick Verice and his company had planned to help with their technology wouldn't see a thing for two decades. And Uconic would be locked into a lucrative but otherwise limiting contract for the whole time.

It was all so familiar, Alex wanted to vomit.

She'd looked into Roderick Verice. He was a good man. A very good man. There was nothing in his history that would suggest he would resort to stealing Abbey Cooper's arm. But then there was little in Alex's own history to suggest she would kill two Russian agents and become a fugitive in her own country.

Life was weird.

And oddly repetitive.

She was rolling with the hunch that if Verice had something here, it was locked away and well hidden. That eliminated everything spread out on the various tables, which she'd been able to see and study from the 3D scans.

She started with the book cases, pulling books and models out as she went. She opened drawers and cabinet doors. She shuffled through every space she opened.

She stopped when she came to the hidden door.

It was a section of wall between two bookcases, continuing a pattern of wainscoting from around the room. A framed painting hung on the wall, just above that wainscoting.

From any casual observation, it was just another segment of the wall. But Alex had studied this space, and the schematics for this floor. She hadn't noticed at first, but now she saw the signs. The room wasn't as wide as it was supposed to be. And here, between two book cases and sets of cabinets, was a space just the right size to be the entry to another part of the room.

She ran her hands over it, looking for anything that might trigger it. She felt around the painting, lifting it from the wall to look behind it. She felt along the wainscoting. She even started pulling books, hoping to find a trigger, just like in the movies.

No luck.

This was a high-end technology firm, though. If there was no mechanical means of opening that door, then that meant there must be some *electronic* means.

She took out her phone and started looking at everything she could find in the company's security database. The entire security grid was open to her. Nothing could stay hidden from QuIEK, once Alex knew it existed.

But most things weren't labeled in a way that made any intuitive sense.

Doorways and security checkpoints were labeled with alphanumeric sequences. She might be able to correlate these with a building schematic, but it was going to take time.

What if she just used a brute force approach?

It was going to be chaotic. And it would put a timer on her window to explore this place further. But it could certainly speed things up.

She used QuIEK to open every door in the building, all at once.

She was sure this would cause some chaos among the security staff, which might lead someone to check in on this space sooner rather than later. But the maneuver had at least paid off in that the door in front of her clicked and opened inward. She pushed her way inside and stopped to take everything in.

It was a clean room, and everywhere she looked were illuminated displays containing bits of technology, a laptop, lockboxes of files, and...

She blinked to see it. Like uncovering the Holy Grail in a glowing temple.

The arm.

Abbey Cooper's arm.

Alex checked the base and the spire of metal that was holding the arm aloft. There was no security on it. The arm was just sitting there, suspended above a cubed surface with a cable running to its charger.

She unzipped a pocket on the leg of her pants and pulled out a bag. It was a simple, packable backpack, with two cords that both cinched the bag closed at the top and then functioned as shoulder straps. Alex picked up the arm and its charger and shoved both into the bag, slinging it over her shoulders and cinching it tight.

She'd done it.

She'd not only figured out who had taken the arm, she'd gotten her hands on the arm itself.

One objective down.

Now there was just one more thing she needed to find, and she knew exactly where it would be.

She went to the laptop, at the center of the clean room, and opened it, turning it on. It was air-gapped—meaning it had never been connected to a wireless signal and was therefore completely secure. Unless, of course, someone broke into the super secret room where it was being kept and used it directly.

It had some pretty sophisticated encryption on it as well, so that even if someone did happen to swipe it, they'd be blocked from any access to it. Very impressive. Military-grade security, for sure. It would definitely keep someone's prying eyes off of the data.

Unless, of course, that someone had QuIEK.

Alex unlocked the system and started rifling through the files. She created a wireless connection to her phone and started wholesale copying the hard drive to Smokescreen. There might be data she'd need to sift through later. But for the moment, she'd spotted what she was looking for.

Documentation for the UPPX prototype. Written in Chinese.

She used a translator app to read some of the file, holding her phone so the camera could see the screen. She verified what she had here, and there was no question what it meant.

Adrian Ballard might have sold out Populus and his government to the Russians, but Roderick Verice was selling out to the Chinese.

Alex snapped pictures of the file just for convenience, and as soon as everything was copied to Smokescreen she set a timer. In just a few hours, unless she decided otherwise, all of these files would be sent to the FBI. Specifically, they'd arrive in the inbox of Agent Eric Symon. Alex felt confident he'd know what they meant, and what to do with them.

There was a sound from outside of the clean room. Alex tucked her phone back into her pocket and zipped it closed. She tightened the straps on the backpack and crept slowly forward.

Two security guards were in the outer room, moving slowly toward the clean room, with weapons drawn. Alex stepped out of the hidden doorway with her hands up.

"Don't move!"

"Hi guys," Alex said. "Listen, I really do believe in

everyone getting a fair shake, so I want to give you a heads up. Your boss is in a lot of trouble."

"Get down on the floor!"

"Ok," Alex said, kneeling on one knee.

"All the way down! Face down!"

Alex leaned forward, as if she were about to comply, and then quickly rotated on her knee, striking out with her other leg and catching the closest guard with a leg sweep. He went down with a yelp, landing on his back directly in front of his partner.

Alex didn't waste a second. She rolled and sprang upward, grabbing the wrist of the hand that was holding the weapon, and then using her body weight to twist his arm outward while she grabbed the gun itself. Her finger blocked his from squeezing, and she bent the gun back and away, bending his trigger finger painfully. He cried out as he released the weapon, and Alex used the butt of it to bludgeon him across the bridge of his nose. He swooned, stunned, and she then kicked him in the knee to send him sprawling on top of his partner.

The other man had been working to get back to his feet, and now found himself laid out on the floor once again, with the weight of the second guard pinning him in place.

Alex took the cuffs out of the second guard's belt, along with the pair she'd kept as a "souvenir" from her near-capture at Shorelite. She cuffed both men wrist to wrist around the thick leg of a heavy credenza, criss-crossing their arms to make it difficult for either to move. She removed their belts and kicked those and the guards' weapons into the clean room, then used QuIEK to close the door behind her.

In a moment she was out of the room and racing toward the back stairs, the same set where she'd run into Roderick Verice during her first infiltration of the Uconic offices. She sprinted down the stairs at a dangerous pace, but stopped three flights up from the lobby.

She pushed through the doors here and raced to the far end of the room. This was a suite of administrative and HR offices, and she passed dozens of cubicles decorated with photos and art and *tchotchkes*.

Alex felt a brief pang of guilt and regret, aware that her work here tonight was going to cost many of these people their jobs.

Justice for one sometimes meant trouble for someone else, she knew.

She'd have to do something for them—somehow make this right for them. A gesture she could make from off-site, though. Far, far from here.

She found the door she was looking for and had it open in a second.

This floor connected to a corridor that was just off of a sky bridge. The walkway crossed the busy street, and as Alex ran, she could see cars racing under, as well as brightly lit billboards and the occasional neon sign stretching off to the horizon.

It made for a surreal run through the glass corridor, like being part of some sort of sci-fi landscape.

The other end of the sky bridge led to a parking garage, where there were more security personnel.

Alex stopped several feet from the doors leading to the garage, next to one of the heavy metal stanchions used to hold up a sign that announced building activities and new employee programs. She reached into another zippered pocket of her pants and took out her new Swiss Army knife. She opened the little Philips-head screwdriver from the back of the knife and held the knife in her fist with the screwdriver sticking out between her fingers—like a set of brass knuckles.

She reared back and struck the glass of the window as hard as she could, making only a small chip. Tiny, spider-web looking cracks started to expand outward from it, though they stopped only millimeters from the chip itself.

It would have to be enough.

She tucked the knife back into her pocket, then backed away from the glass. She took a breath, and then raced forward, leaping into a flying kick, landing hard against the window, her leading foot striking the zone with the chip and cracks dead center.

The impact did its work. A larger web of cracks spread from the small divot, spreading along the glass in long streaks.

Alex picked up the metal stanchion, hefted it like a sledgehammer, and then smashed it into the glass.

Once. Twice. Three times, and suddenly the glass shattered, falling away to the street below. Alex swept at the jagged opening, clearing a path, and then tossed the stanchion aside. She peered out over the street, took a breath, and then jumped.

She landed on the roof of the RV, slipping a bit on the white surface but steadying herself with a hand on one of the air conditioner units. She then scrambled for the ladder at the back of the RV, sliding down it and hitting the ground with a thud.

She ran then, passing the RV and taking note of the parking violation sticker on the driver-side window as she sprinted by. She'd square that with the rental place. She'd already left a serious wad of cash inside for their trouble.

A block or so away, she ducked into the alley between the parking garage and the building next to it. Here she recovered the bag she'd stashed, and changed clothes, stuffing the light backpack and its contents into a canvas gym bag. She then climbed over the short wall of the parking garage, landing on the pavement next to the Lexus.

She was inside and moving out of the ground level exit in moments. She had arranged for the garage cameras to shut down for the evening, so she wouldn't be burning this car just yet. In fact, all the local cameras—from building security to ATMs—had mysteriously malfunctioned during this time.

Out on the street she could already hear police sirens approaching. She'd have to start making turns and navigating to her next waypoint, but all the attention from the police was on the opposite side of the structure she'd just left. There was no one here to spot her.

She was clear.

It was going to be a long night of switching rides and changing clothes, but it was worth it. She'd already set all of that up, so now it was just down to seeing the plans through.

Tomorrow, Abbey Cooper would get her arm back.

The job would be done.

And Alex would soon be gone.

CHAPTER TWENTY-ONE

It was 6 AM, and Mayher met Symon in the lobby, just as they'd planned.

He was holding the warrant. He'd stayed up half the night working to expedite it, calling the local Director in the middle of the evening, waking up judges, hurrying through more than twenty pages of justification for the action. But he had it. He had the warrant. The rushed work had put it in his hands by 5 AM.

By 6 AM it was a worthless piece of paper.

He felt like crap and he was sure that feeling was just getting started.

Mayher, a bit bleary-eyed herself, poured a cup of complimentary coffee from a large urn in the lobby. She held the cup up, offering, and Symon accepted.

"So it all went down last night," Mayher said, pulling another cup. "And we missed it."

"Worse," Symon said, scowling. "She emailed me."

"What did she say?" Mayher asked, taking a gingerly sip.

"See for yourself," he replied, handing her his phone.

Mayher took it and looked it over, swiping through the email, the attachments, the photos.

"Holy shit!"

"Yeah. She handed us the whole thing. Everything we need to take down Roderick Verice and Uconic. I've already got two agents bringing him in. We'll be raiding the facility this morning, before the employees even get there."

Mayher handed the phone back to him. "And Alex Kayne?"

He made a sour face. "What do you think?"

"Already in the wind?"

He shook his head. "I can't doubt it. But just in case, I have people watching Abbey Cooper's apartment, her workplace, a few other locations."

Mayher looked dubious. "She's too smart for that."

Symon shrugged, and despite himself he gave a quirky half smile. "Have to try. The police interviewed the two guards she trussed up on one of the upper floors. They reported a secret room that we'll be turning upside down. I'm betting the one thing we won't find there is Abbey Cooper's prosthetic arm."

"So we're banking on Alex trying to return it."

"It's our last lead," Symon shrugged. "In the meantime, she may be in the wind but she did hand us everything we need to clear this cold case."

Mayher thought this over. "Would you hold it against me if I said I kind of hate her but I kind of like her?"

"How could I?" Symon asked, sipping his coffee as he led Mayher out through the glass doors of the hotel, into the Orlando morning as the sun was just starting to rise.

"I feel the same way."

THEY WERE WATCHING.

Of *course* they were watching.

There was no chance that Alex was going to get the arm to Abbey by simply walking in and handing it to her. There wasn't a disguise on Earth that was good enough to make that possible.

Luckily, Roderick Verice had given her an alternative method.

Alex was sitting in a cafe, miles away from the scene, though she had eyes on the place. She had a grid of live security and traffic footage on her laptop screen.

She watched, and when she saw that it was time, she called the burner phone.

Once the connection was made, she was able to turn on the GoPro she'd attached to the arm. This was going to be...

Well, *interesting* was maybe the best way to describe it, though that didn't quite do the job.

A little fun. A little weird. A *lot* weird.

Alex had made things a little easier by placing the arm on a skateboard and letting it drag itself in a grasp-glide-grasp method. This also felt less creepy than the Adam's Family-esque "Thing" crawl, fingers flexing while dragging the arm along the ground, behind.

The arm and power supply were light enough that the arm's own motive power was plenty to get it going at a decent speed. In fact, it was kind of fun to watch it skitter along, pausing to hide itself in bushes or behind trash cans or under cars parked on the street.

Watching and navigating via the GoPro was a bit disorienting, and Alex frequently glanced at the other cameras, observing and double-checking as the arm emerged from behind the garage of the building across the street. It glided across the street in seconds and rolled down the sidewalk straight toward Abbey's building.

Alex checked the cameras that were oriented on that spot. Abbey had exited her apartment a few minutes before Alex had gotten things moving, and she'd just turned onto the walkway when she stopped... staring.

Alex smiled, letting the arm glide forward a bit before using its fingers to slow to a stop. She then made the hand rise, waving and flexing its fingers.

She called the burner phone she'd sent to Abbey.

"H-hello?" Abbey answered.

"Hello, Abbey," Alex replied, smiling. "I think this belongs to you."

"Oh my God," Abbey whispered. "You did it. You... actually *did it!*"

Abbey stooped, opening the buckles of the straps Alex had used to put the arm on the skateboard. She detached the power supply, and shrugged off the light jacket she'd been wearing, letting it fall to the ground. She then attached the arm, and Alex smiled again to see Abbey flex and move it, getting the feel for something she'd lost not once but twice.

"It's a freaking miracle!" Abbey shouted, raising the arm in a victory cheer.

Alex laughed. "They happen. Sometimes. But listen, I want you to do me a favor."

"Anything! Thank you!"

"You're welcome, Abbey," Alex smiled. "But when you talk about this, to the press or whoever, I want you to tell them that it was Agents Eric Symon and Julia Mayher, from the FBI, that recovered the arm and got it back to you."

"Symon... The agent who came to my work?" Abbey asked.

"Yeah, that's the one," Alex smiled. "And his partner is Agent Mayher. Can you remember to do that for me?"

Abbey laughed. "You don't really work for the FBI, do you?"

"I told you," Alex replied, "I'm a free agent. But... I think I'll be doing more work with the FBI in the future."

EPILOGUE

THE STORY WAS BIG. National news. And that worked out pretty well for Symon.

His superiors were far more generous over his failure to bring in Alex Kayne with a big, positive news story making the rounds. They made it clear that they still expected him to do the job, but he had some breathing room for the moment. Good press, especially after a few recent black eyes to the Bureau, came with at least a little leeway.

True to her pattern, Alex disappeared after managing to return Abbey's arm. They'd watched the whole thing play out from local security footage, and one of Symon's agents had been on the scene, nearby. He had reported seeing nothing at all, except that Abbey Cooper had answered a cell phone, then stooped down to pick up the arm.

There'd been no sign of Alex Kayne. And retrieving and scanning the burner phone had led exactly nowhere.

For all Symon knew, Alex might have been in a whole other city when she'd made the arm deliver itself to Abbey Cooper. With QuIEK, Kayne could extend her virtual presence to nearly anywhere. No need to risk getting snagged. She could just as easily have done the work from somewhere offsite, maybe even from another state.

Symon was going to be in another state soon, himself. He was wrapping up some of the details of this case with the Orlando home office Director, and that meant his time here was done.

At least he'd had a chance to see Disney World. Thanks to Kayne giving him the runaround, of course.

It wasn't all bad news, then.

In fact, he'd gotten an email from Director Elizabeth Ludlum, at the Manhattan FBI offices. She was heading something new—a whole new branch of federal law enforcement, from the sound of it. Something called *Historic Crimes*. Would he be willing to chat with her?

He would, indeed. From the brief write-up she sent him, which had included temporary access to the agent portal on the website at HistoricCrimes.com, Symon had gathered that this was something new and interesting. He had no idea what Director Ludlum wanted to talk to him about, but he was intrigued.

In the meantime, he finished the debriefing with the Orlando Director, then gathered what few things he had in his borrowed cubicle and made his exit.

He was just slipping behind the wheel of his car when his mobile phone rang.

The mobile phone.

"Agent Symon," he answered cautiously.

"Nice job, Eric," she said from the other side.

"I could say the same to you, Ms. Kayne," he said.

"Oh, are we back to being formal? I was kind of hoping we'd gotten to a new level in our relationship. What with us working so well together."

"That was a one-off," Symon said. "Unless you'd like to turn yourself in? You know, I might actually be able to pull some strings, get some special consideration. You could become an FBI asset, maybe..."

She laughed, a sharp bark as if she might have been taken by surprise. "Eric, come on. We both know you don't have any strings to pull. Not after everything that happened."

She was right, of course. He was lucky to even have his job. He had virtually no pull with the Bureau, at this point, and the only reason he was here now was because he was actually pretty good at finding people like Alex Kayne.

Or used to be. Maybe he was slipping.

"Besides," Alex continued, "I'm too high profile to get that kind of deal. I'm a traitor to my country, remember? A murderer and a traitor."

"You're not wrong," he said. "It wouldn't be as simple as raising your hands and coming clean. But this... this was actually a good start... Alex."

He could hear the smile in her voice when she spoke. "A good start. Ok. Well, that has a nice ring to it. You think we'll be working together again in the future, Eric?"

It was his turn to smile. "If you're not turning yourself in, I expect we'll be bumping into each other again at some point." He thought for a moment, started the car and put it in gear as he clicked his seatbelt around him. He had to get to the airport. He needed to get back to his own office, his own home, take care of his own life for a minute. Plants to water, mail to open, that sort of thing.

He figured Alex Kayne would lie low for just a little while, and he needed to regroup. "Listen," he said, "for what it's worth..." He hesitated.

"Yeah?" Alex asked, curious.

He exhaled, then said, "I do believe you're innocent."

There was a long pause from the other end of the line, and Symon fished his ear buds out of a pocket, popping them in so he could be hands-free as he drove. He pulled out of the parking lot of Orlando's FBI headquarters and onto the street.

"Thanks, Eric. It means a lot. It's not enough, of course. But it means a lot."

He nodded. "I know," he said. "I have to bring you in, if I can. You understand that, right? We're... we're not friends."

"No, I guess we're not. And yeah, I do understand. But keep that phone, ok?"

He smiled. "Ok, Alex. And I'm going to be the one to arrest you. You should also know that."

"Never had a doubt," Alex replied, and the call ended.

He shook his head, then pulled the earbuds out of his ears and tossed them along with the phone into the little cubby under the car's radio.

"Alex Kayne," he said, shaking his head again. He laughed and then smiled all the way to the airport.

"Agent Eric Symon," Alex said, shaking her head and laughing lightly.

She watched his car grow smaller in the distance, turning under an overpass and disappearing from sight.

She glanced around, taking things in.

There was a little sign in front of her, only a few feet away, that warned people to be cautious of snakes and alligators.

It was funny how a place like this, surrounded by some of the best examples of modern society, could somehow still include hidden dangers like snakes and alligators. Right here, hidden in plain sight, there could be something waiting.

The little pond by the Federal building was serene and calm, and that made it deceptive.

She walked back to the Lexus, parked in the shade. She climbed in, got the air conditioner going at push-the-heat-back levels, and got moving.

Tomorrow she'd trade the Lexus for something more discreet, and by the end of the day she'd be in another state entirely. She'd already picked out the next client, and he was far from here.

That was good. Far from here was good.

But for now, Alex had earned herself a little rest and vacation. And with the FBI so cock-sure that she couldn't *possibly* still be in Orlando, this had become the absolute safest place for her to be.

So she might as well take one last run at Disney World.

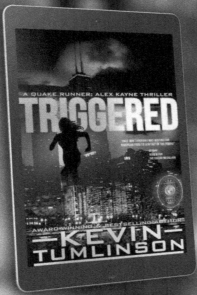

A NOTE AT THE END

Well, hello there.

I'm going to be honest—I'm not entirely sure where to start with this particular "Note at the End."

If you've read any of my other books, you're already familiar with how this usually goes: The story's done. The threads are (mostly) tied off. There's a promise of more to come. And now we chat. Just me and you.

If you're new to this, you may not get it, but stick with me. This is the part of the book where I do a little free-range roaming, and sometimes I actually say things that are worth reading.

You can skip this whole section, though, if this stuff bores you. But I hope you'll stick around, anyway. If you just read the whole book, this is a chance to peek into the brain of the guy who wrote it, and I'd love to get to know you

(In fact... if you like this sort of thing, be sure to get on my email list at https://kevintumlinson.com/joinme. I send my readers stuff like this all the time!)

Anyway, here we are, at the end of the very first "Quake Runner" novel. We've met Alex Kayne—fugitive and genius.

We've met Agent Eric Symon—sharp and dedicated Federal Agent, though with a blemish or two on his record. No fault of his own.

I have a confession to make about this book: It wasn't meant to be self-published.

Which may shock some people, because self-publishing/indie-publishing is kind of my thing. Not only have I done it successfully since 2008, but I've also been a big advocate for the indie publishing community. I have a popular podcast aimed at that audience, and I help with marketing and PR for the leading ebook distributor online and worldwide. I'm even known as "the Voice of Indie Publishing."

So self-publishing is kind of a big deal for me. And deciding to go the traditional route is a bit unusual. But I did have my reasons.

I wrote the first draft of this book more than two years ago, by special request. A literary agent, who shall not be named, had read and liked my work, and was interested in representing me. But she had been "burned" by a deal with another self-published author, also not to be named, whose ego got a little bigger than it should have.

So tempted to name names. *Must... resist...*

When this (very nice, and very respectable) agent reached out to me, I was definitely intrigued. I'd had my swing at a traditional contract, way back in 2006, and things had gone pear shaped with that deal. It had cost me a bit of money out of pocket to resolve the whole thing, and I had seriously thought my writing career was over before it had begun.

Self-publishing had amped up around that time, however, and it had given me a chance to build the career I always wanted. Which, of course, I did.

There's something about self-publishing that's simply empowering. Also, lucrative. You, the author, are in control of your fate and destiny, and there are no gatekeepers to prevent you from going as far as you want, as fast as you want. You own the whole business.

Of course... you *own the whole business*. Which means that not only are the books your responsibility, so is the marketing and the production work (getting a cover, hiring editors, managing launches, and on and on). You get to completely own your intellectual property and decide what to do with it, which is a plus. But if the book fails, that's also on you.

So... no pressure.

I love owning every aspect of my books, and I've had a lot of success since getting into this business. I don't even mind marketing, though I'll be the first to admit I could be better at it. So I'm pro-self-publishing, all the way.

But I'd be lying if I said I'd never consider a traditional book deal. Having someone else take on some of the workload of producing and promoting the books would be heavenly, especially if I *made* money from the deal, rather than *spend* money on it.

I'm a very tough negotiator when it comes to my intellec-tual property rights, though, so any deal I enter into is going to involve a lot of concessions from the publisher. Which means getting a deal in the first place is a bit unlikely.

So when Agent X (as we'll call her) told me that she was interested, but wanted to see something new, original, and not previously published, I decided, "What the heck?"

I'd give it a whirl.

I was doing a lot of traveling for author conferences at the time that Agent X reached out to me, and a lot of that was focused on Orlando. In fact, when this whole offer came through, I was literally sitting in a restaurant connected to a Disney Resort, on a layover between two Florida conferences, and I had some time to kill.

I love Disney World, maybe even more than the next guy. But when you're there by yourself for a week—well, there are only so many rides and so many shows a guy can take before he just wants to sit down for some non-Mouse-related quiet time.

So, I started writing. And because Orlando and Disney were fresh on my mind, I set my story there.

True confession #2: I actually had the concept for this book (and the series) mapped out ahead of time, before Agent X ever reached out to me.

That story requires looping back a bit.

In 2016, my wife and I had sold our home and bought an RV, so we could travel full time while I attended author conferences and book signings, and generally just researched ideas for my archaeological thriller series (and whatever other books I wanted to write). During that time, on top of figuring out how to live on the road, I also learned about an opportunity to co-author with thriller author James Patterson.

The opportunity came to me through Master Class—the online series of courses hosted by celebrities in a variety of disciplines. James Patterson was, as far as I recall, the first writer to be invited into Master Class. And a thriller writer, at that. So I was onboard. I was excited to see what I could learn from one of the most prolific and wealthy thriller writers on the planet.

As a paying student for Patterson's Master Class, you were given a special offer—you could pitch an idea and, potentially, win a chance to put what you'd learned from Patterson to work, penning a new book based on your concept.

It was a great opportunity—Patterson is a master of marketing. He's essentially a self-publisher with a traditional deal. And I figured that even though I wasn't exactly floundering to get started in my author career, it couldn't hurt to have my name and work associated with Patterson's. It might help bump me to the next level.

There was very little to lose, but a whole lot to gain.

So, I wrote up a concept, fleshed it out, and sent it in. And then I waited.

The competition ran for a couple of months, and in the end my concept was reviewed and then...!

Rejected.

Actually, to be honest, since I got no feedback whatsoever I can't even be sure Patterson ever saw it. Maybe he did, or maybe he didn't. But at any rate, my concept was not chosen, and so I didn't get to work with Patterson.

Whether that was a good thing or a bad thing, I can't honestly say. But I never considered it wasted effort. Ideas are easy, and explaining them is both fun and useful—it helps sharpen the writing tool in your brain, when you have to give someone a fully-fleshed-out idea. I don't do this, typically, when I'm writing a book. So it was an exercise in something new that ended up teaching me a lot.

Plus, I got a well-shaped series concept out of it.

I put the idea aside, thinking, "Someday I'll write this."

The idea sat on my hard drive for a couple of years, then. Not quite out of mind—I would occasionally revisit it, wondering about it, making sure it was still there, in a sense. Was I still interested in it? Yes. Did I want to write it now? Not yet. Patience, young story. Shhh. You'll have your day.

And on it went, until it became "the story I'll get to, at some point." I'll admit, I felt a twinge of guilt over it. Because that's what writers do. If we think of something, but we don't write it, something within us gnaws at our very soul, sucking the marrow from our bones, stooping us over like old men playing chess in the park. If we never write that story, it becomes a "coulda been."

"It coulda been a great book!" Ancient Kevin proclaims. Check!

"But I didn't get around to writing it!" Check mate.

And another danger: The story might get tired of waiting for me, and go somewhere else.

Sound nuts? I always thought so, too. But then I read Elizabeth Gilbert's "Big Magic," wherein she talks about ideas coming to creatives, offering themselves up like maidens at a debutante's ball. Are you the suitor of their dreams? Will you take their hand and dance?

Offers such as these are only good for a limited time. As Elizabeth Gilbert explained it, eventually the ideas move on and go to someone else. They'll be patient, for a time. You were their first choice. They think you'd do great. But if you don't act...

Working in a creative field is weird, right?

But it is true, that if an author doesn't eventually put an idea to use, it will definitely be out of reach. Either the idea will become stale, and the author no longer wants to explore it at all, or the author dies or otherwise becomes unavailable. Morbid, but true.

So when Agent X came around, asking what I had in my bin that might make for a good pitch, I figured there was enough of a cosmic convergence that I should dust off that old treatment and get to work.

If you're new to my books, there's a sometimes startling fact you'll need to know about me: Most of my books are written in about 15 days.

That's not to say I don't spend time doing rewrites and edits, which can expand a book's production outward to the 30-40 day mark. It's just that my first drafts tend to be done in just a few weeks.

Once that draft is done, I edit, and I recruit others to edit as well. My early work lacked some professional luster, from time to time, but since I've started making my living from these books, I've put more and more resources into making them as perfect as they can be.

And I fall short of perfection every time, of course. Dozens of passes, hundreds of sets of eyes, and large wads of money, and there are still typos. Just fewer typos than I had ten years ago or even five years ago.

This book, like most, was originally written in one of those 15-day stretches. The first draft started while I was in Orlando, and was finished in San Francisco, before I took it back to Sugar Land, Texas. In between, I'm pretty sure there were at least two other cities and states. It was a busy 15 days.

But there I was. Book done. Ready for edit. Ready to send to Agent X!

And I stopped.

I didn't do the edit. In fact, I saved the file and went on to write six more books in my *Dan Kotler Archaeological Thrillers,* over the next two years. I moved three times, including getting off of the road and into a couple of different apartments. I traveled to a dozen more cities for a dozen more conferences. I even sent the book to a different agent who read it, liked it, and gave me notes on it.

But that was as far as I went.

Until a week ago, when I dusted it off, read it, edited it, and then started writing this Note at the End.

So... why?

Why did I choose to hold back this book, instead of running with it? Why did I decide not to send it to Agent X, after all? Or back to that other agent, who seemed interested as well? Or do anything at all with it, really?

Honestly, I don't have a good answer.

Except...

Except it didn't feel like *the right time*.

It wasn't *this book's* time.

I know that sounds crazy. It was written. Offers were tentatively made. But until a week ago, when I'd finished the eleventh Dan Kotler book (*The God Resurrection*), and was contemplating what to do next, I really just didn't have a strong feeling about moving forward with this book.

But then, in that 11th Kotler book, I did something I've been thinking about for years. I took the idea of *Historic Crimes*, my fictional law enforcement task force that gave anthropologist Dan Kotler an excuse to work with FBI Agent Roland Denzel, and I upgraded it to a full-fledged but still fictional federal law enforcement agency, with one of my through-line characters put in charge.

You may have noticed a mention of this in the Epilogue of this book.

Historic Crimes changes everything.

For the past half-decade, I've been focused entirely on writing thrillers. More to the point, I've focused entirely on writing a *specific series* of thrillers. And I love them. I love Dr. Dan Kotler and Agent Roland Denzel. I love Dr. Liz Ludlum and Agent Dani Brown. I love the ever-evolving cast of supporting characters, and the ongoing search through archaeological dig sites and "out-of-place history" that feed the plots of these books. But I have ideas for other stories, too. Stories that wouldn't fit in a Dan Kotler book.

With the creation of Historic Crimes, I have an opportunity.

All of my books are set in the same universe—more or less. I have a series of YA fantasy novels called *Sawyer Jackson* that actually does some universe hopping. But every book I've ever published has, secreted within it, some breadcrumb or Easter egg that ties it to every single other book I've written.

That said, one thing I've learned about readers is that they tend to want to stick with a certain series, and aren't necessarily willing to follow the author on whatever weird side-trip he or she wishes to make.

This is why an author can have a mega-hit bestseller one year and then lose the audience on the next book. People want to see more Jack Reacher, or more Harry Potter, or more Robert Langdon. Divergence is only mildly tolerated (just like the movie based on the book of that title... *badump-bump, zing!*).

This is a dilemma for writers. Because, on the one hand, if we didn't *like* the characters and stories we created, we wouldn't have created them in the first place.

But you can really *like* making clam chowder and still want to make tacos from time to time.

The trouble is, even though I, the author, am free to write whatever I wish, the reader, who is free to read whatever *they* wish, may not follow me into those brave, new worlds. And since I need readers to actually *buy* the books if I want to continue eating, I must deliver what they expect.

Within reason.

As an author, I do feel a certain obligation to meet reader expectations, to a point. After all, if they came in loving Dan Kotler, and I suddenly turn Dan Kotler into a robot who lives on a distant world, and who pines for the day when he can become a real boy, I'm going to lose some folks.

I have to deliver Kotler stories that actually are Kotler stories.

My hope, however, is that people who read my Kotler stories will also want to read other adventures, with other characters, doing other things.

This was one of the reasons I started writing some B and C stories in my books, to accompany the A story about Kotler and Denzel and whatever case they were working. Dr. Liz Ludlum and Agent Dani Brown became protagonists in their own rights, with stories that were only tangentially connected to the main story. And in this way, I was (I hoped) introducing the reader to the idea that other things are going on in this universe I've created. There are other stories here, that might be just as interesting as what Dan Kotler was up to.

That's the goal, anyway. And I took great care to lay the groundwork for this so I could start writing books with different themes and plots from what I'd written before.

It's entirely possible that if I write more thrillers, readers might come along. It's also possible that if those aren't Dan Kotler thrillers, I'll lose them.

My solution to this, though, was to introduce the idea of Historic Crimes.

The name came up early in the Dan Kotler series and was really more of a convenience than the intentional early seed of a new era. I needed an excuse to have Dan Kotler getting involved in FBI cases on a regular basis, and for the FBI to care about moldy old tombs and ancient artifacts when there are terrorist plots and murders to solve.

Historic Crimes was the bridge between these two worlds.

As time went by, however, I started to realize that this absurd, impossible FBI task force might have more uses than simply being a convenient trope. In fact, it might provide my salvation.

Over the course of several books, I started expanding on Historic Crimes. I gave it some back story, and some challenges. I brought in characters who could focus on it, while Kotler and Denzel focused on whatever the current case (the "A story") was.

Basically, I created a mythos and an infrastructure. And then, when it was ready, I made it "a thing."

Is it plausible or realistic to think that a brand new law

enforcement agency might be founded, with the express purpose of policing history-related crimes?

Eh.

Probably not.

But it's not *impossible*, if the conditions are right. And I created conditions that would make it something a bit *more* plausible, at least.

Some readers are going to balk at the idea, which I completely understand. Some already have, "patiently" explaining to me (usually in negative reviews) that "this isn't how this works." I do get that. I'm making some of this up as I go.

But because I've done the footwork, this implausible idea becomes plausible *within the universe I created.*

That may sound a bit convenient. But I hereby invoke the ancient right of Creators: Our universe, our rules.

Thanks to the groundwork I've done, I can now start expanding on that universe.

You'll note, I'm sure, that *Quake Runner* is not "history-related." But as things progress with Historic Crimes, the charter for this fledgling agency is going to see some... tweaks and expansions.

I have plans.

You're just going to have to trust me.

For now, though, the birth of this new federal agency gives me enough of an excuse to bring this book, which languished for years on my hard drive, into the light of day. The time was finally right. And I think it was worth the wait.

Alex Kayne is a brilliant character. I love her with fire in my heart.

I wanted to write a female protagonist who was not the *typical* female protagonist. I wanted her to be tough and smart —the old standbys used to describe literally every female hero.

But I also wanted her to be independent, autonomous, self-empowered, and above all, *real*.

So many female protagonists are portrayed as basically "men with boobs." Sorry for the mildly offensive imagery.

Or, worse, they're portrayed as "vulnerable" to the point of being ineffective, and yet they somehow manage to succeed, anyway, as if "girl power" was some kind of *deus ex machina*. I hate that one. A lot. Just *being* female isn't a super power. Strength comes from individuality, not cultural identity.

Likewise, I hate the way most media has portrayed "strong" female characters as essentially amped-up chick-lit protagonists, as if every woman is out there making rain, but really wishes they could just settle down.

"She's a tough, smart woman... who could really use a good man in her life."

Holy crap.

Have these people ever actually *met* a woman? Or a human?

When I created Alex Kayne, I intentionally aimed for her to be smarter than everyone else, but still make dumb mistakes. Her "vulnerability" isn't her femininity, in other words. It's her *humanity*.

Does Alex need Agent Eric Symon, the big-strong man, to help get her out of a fix?

Sometimes.

And sometimes, *he needs her*.

Is Alex Kayne an indefatigable, unstoppable fighting machine, capable of taking anyone (especially a *man*) in a fight?

No.

She's pretty good, though. Better than most people. She's trained, and she knows how to handle herself. Her genitalia doesn't prevent her from that, but it also doesn't grant her a ridiculous level of super stamina and strength. She'll take her lumps, just like anyone else. And when she comes back, it's like every underdog, *Cinderella Man* story: She succeeds because of her *indomitable spirit* and her *resourcefulness,* not because she's a she.

Is Alex Kayne smarter than all men everywhere, forever and ever, because *girl power?*

Well... sort of.

But only in that she's pretty much smarter than everyone in general (including me... I constantly have to look stuff up).

Girl power? No.

Individual power? Hell yes.

How could I write a female character at all, if the only quality of strength she had was her gender? I do not, in any sense, buy into the joke of "cultural appropriation" or the idea that "only someone from IDENTITY X can legitimately write from the point of view of IDENTITY X." That's a huge load of cow crap, right there.

But I can write humans. I can write individuals. I can write about people who face challenges that are bigger and scarier than they want to face, and tell you how those people would react. Because I happen to be a people.

So my last true confession for this note: I named her Alex Kayne on purpose. Meaning, I intentionally gave her a "male" name.

And, addendum to true confession: She didn't actually start off as a woman.

At least, in *this book* she didn't start as a woman, though in the original concept she always was.

I decided in the original concept that I was going to create a female protagonist, but when I started writing the actual book I had set the character's gender as male. I can't really explain why, except to say that I'd had great success writing male characters, and had not, to that point, written a great many female leads. What few I did write, however, had been well-received. And over time, I did develop a few who, I believe and have been told, have been remarkably good and even inspiring characters.

But when I was asked to pitch something new, I balked. I defaulted back to the male protagonist. I... think I was trying to "play it safe."

I didn't get far, though.

I think by the end of the first chapter, I'd already decided that Alex had to be a *she*.

There was something about the character that just demanded it.

And wow, am I glad I listened. Because once Alex Kayne was on the page, I fell in love with her. Completely and totally.

She broke every stereotype I could think of. She remained vulnerable, but refused to let that vulnerability either define her or be a weakness. In fact, she often used that vulnerability as a source of strength.

I could have told this story with a male protagonist. There may have been some slight variations in the character, but he would have mostly stayed the same.

But sometimes the character *tells you* who they are. And that's exactly what happened with Alex Kayne.

She *demanded* that she was female. And so she was.

And I'm really glad of it, because I think she's amazing. She brings together all the best qualities of all the most incredible and amazing women who have been a part of my life, including my much-loved grandmother, Sammie Mansel.

You'll note the "male" name. It's not short for "Samantha." She was born "Sammie," and I couldn't imagine a better fitting name. She owned it. She made it mean something that goes beyond gender.

I've always been her biggest fan, even now that she's gone.

You might also note the relationship between Alex Kayne and her Papa.

This was a bit of a juxtaposition of genders, as a way of illustrating my own relationship with my Granny. A huge influence in my life, and a source of strength for me even now, decades after she passed away.

Alex Kayne isn't me. I want to make that clear, for whoever may be playing amateur psychoanalyst in the room. Alex isn't some subconscious yearning on my part, or an expression of some repressed desire.

She isn't anyone but Alex Kayne. Her own being. Strong, smart, and all her.

I do, however, see within Alex some of my DNA, as well as the wisdom I learned from my grandmother and the rest of my beloved family and friends.

Alex has got all the right chops.

I loved writing about her. Loved it. And can't wait to write more.

But here we are, then. At the end of the first book. The end of the beginning.

I can promise there are more stories about Alex Kayne on the way. She hasn't had her last run-in with Agent Eric Symon or the FBI. She hasn't cleared her name, and she isn't safe.

She's ready and set.

And now we go.

There will be more stories. More Alex Kayne. More Historic Crimes.

And I can't wait for you to see it all.

Good health and God bless,
  Kevin Tumlinson
  Sugar Land, TX
  May 20, 2020

HERE'S HOW TO HELP ME REACH MORE READERS

If you loved this book, you can help me reach more readers with just a few easy acts of kindness.

(1) REVIEW THIS BOOK

Leaving a review for this book is a great way to help other readers find it. Just go to the site where you bought the book, search for the title, and leave a review. It really helps, and I really appreciate it.

(2) SUBSCRIBE TO MY EMAIL LIST

I regularly write a special email to the people on my list, just keeping everyone up to date on what I'm working on. When I announce new book releases, giveaways, or anything else, the people on my list hear about it first. Sometimes, there are special deals I'll *only* give to my list, so it's worth being a part of the crowd.

Join the conversation and get a free ebook, just for signing up! Visit https://www.kevintumlinson.com/joinme.

(3) TELL YOUR FRIENDS

Word of mouth is still the best marketing there is, so I would greatly appreciate it if you'd tell your friends and family about this book, and the others I've written.

You can find a comprehensive list of all of my books at http://kevintumlinson.com/books.

Thanks so much for your help. And thanks for reading.

ABOUT THE AUTHOR

Kevin Tumlinson is an award-winning and bestselling novelist, living in Texas and working in random coffee shops, cafés, and hotel lobbies worldwide. His debut thriller, *The Coelho Medallion*, was a 2016 Shelf Notable Indie award winner.

Kevin grew up in Wild Peach, Texas, where he was raised by his grandparents and given a healthy respect for story telling. He often found himself in trouble in school for writing stories instead of doing his actual assignments.

Kevin's love for history, archaeology, and science has been a tremendous source of material for his writing, feeding his fiction and giving him just the excuse he needs to read the next article, biography, or research paper.

Connect with Kevin:
kevintumlinson.com
kevin@tumlinson.net

ALSO BY KEVIN TUMLINSON

Dan Kotler

The Coelho Medallion

The Atlantis Riddle

The Devil's Interval

The Girl in the Mayan Tomb

The Antarctic Forgery

The Stepping Maze

The God Extinction

The Spanish Papers

The Hidden Persuaders

The Sleeper's War

The God Resurrection

Dan Kotler Short Fiction

The Brass Hall - A Dan Kotler Story

The Jani Sigil - FREE short story from BookHip.com/DBXDHP

Dan Kotler Box Sets

The Book of Lost Things: Dan Kotler, Books 1-3

The Book of Betrayals: Dan Kotler, Books 4-6

The Book of Gods and Kings: Dan Kotler, Books 7-9

Quake Runner: Alex Kayne

Shaken

Triggered (Forthcoming)

Citadel

Citadel: First Colony

Citadel: Paths in Darkness

Citadel: Children of Light

Citadel: The Value of War

Colony Girl: A Citadel Universe Story

Sawyer Jackson

Sawyer Jackson and the Long Land

Sawyer Jackson and the Shadow Strait

Sawyer Jackson and the White Room

Think Tank

Karner Blue

Zero Tolerance

Nomad

The Lucid — Co-authored with Nick Thacker

Episode 1

Episode 2

Episode 3

Standalone

Evergreen

Shorts & Novellas

Getting Gone

Teresa's Monster

The Three Reasons to Avoid Being Punched in the Face

Tin Man

Two Blocks East

Edge

Zero

Collections & Anthologies

Citadel: Omnibus

Uncanny Divide — With Nick Thacker & Will Flora

Light Years — The Complete Science Fiction Library

Dead of Winter: A Christmas Anthology — With Nick Thacker, Jim Heskett, David Berens, M.P. MacDougall, R.A. McGee, Dusty Sharp & Steven Moore

YA & Middle Grade

Secret of the Diamond Sword — An Alex Kotler Mystery

Wordslinger (Non-Fiction)

30-Day Author: Develop a Daily Writing Habit and Write Your Book In 30 Days (Or Less)

Watch for more at kevintumlinson.com/books

KEEP THE ADVENTURE GOING!

GET MORE THRILLS FROM AWARD-WINNING AND BESTSELLING AUTHOR, KEVIN TUMLINSON!

★★★★★ "Half way through I was waiting for Harrison Ford to leap out of the pages!"
—Deanne, Review for *The Coelho Medallion*

★★★★★ "Kevin has crashed onto the action-thriller scene

as only an action-thriller author can: with provocative plot lines, unforgettable characters, and enough adrenaline to keep you awake all night."
—Nick Thacker, author of *Mark for Blood*

★★★★★ "Move over Daniel Silva, James Patterson, and Dan Brown."
—Chip Polk, Review for *The Atlantis Riddle*

★★★★★ "Move Over Indiana Jones, there is a New Dr. in Town!"
—Cycletrash, Review for *The Coelho Medallion*

★★★★★ "[Kevin Tumlinson] is what every writer should be—entertaining and thought-provoking."
— Shana Tehan, Press Secretary, U.S. House of Representatives

★★★★★ "I discovered Kevin Tumlinson from The Creative Penn podcast and immediately got his novel, Evergreen. I read it in like 3 seconds. It's the most fast-paced story I've encountered."
—R.D. Holland, Independent Reviewer

★★★★★ "Comparison to Clive Cussler is a natural, though Tumlinson's 'Dan ' is more like Dan Brown's Robert Langdon than Dirk Pitt."
—Amazon Review for *The Coelho Medallion*

FIND YOUR NEXT FAVORITE BOOK AT
KevinTumlinson.com/books

CPSIA information can be obtained
at www.ICGtesting.com
Printed in the USA
BVHW082024150920
588775BV00026B/180